CHONTAE CHORCAI
ERVICE RULES

on or

Finger of fate

He had executed the perfect crime. They could search but there would be no fingerprints, no nothing. He had worn gloves, a hat pulled well down ... And he and the woman had no connection. People were such fools, volunteering information to strangers; so many of them did it, which made his plans so much easier. And when the job was finally completed, if – which he doubted – anyone questioned him, he had proof he was not involved. He would also have a perfect alibi.

Debbie Orchard was the first, Victoria Baxter the second. Both strangled.

Detective Chief Inspector Ian Roper at Rickenham Green HQ was baffled. 'We have two victims, both roughly the same age, and both were discovered by their husbands. The odd thing is, both of them allowed their killer in and there're no signs of a struggle.'

Out there was a killer, always one step ahead of the police, coldly ruthless in his deadly expertise. But Roper and his team tirelessly probed for clues until their stubborn patience was rewarded and a strangler, about to strike again, was overpowered.

Pace, tension, clever plotting and characters who leap from the page are what distinguish Janie Bolitho's riveting whodunit.

Also by Janie Bolitho

Kindness can kill (1993)
Ripe for revenge (1994)
Motive for murder (1994)
Dangerous deceit (1995)

FINGER OF FATE

Janie Bolitho

Constable · London

First published in Great Britain 1996
by Constable & Company Ltd
3 The Lanchesters, 162 Fulham Palace Road
London W6 9ER
Copyright © 1996 by Janie Bolitho
The right of Janie Bolitho to be
identified as the author of this work
has been asserted by her in accordance
with the Copyright, Designs and Patents Act 1988
ISBN 0 09 475440 3
Set in Linotron Palatino 10 pt by
CentraCet Limited, Cambridge
Printed and bound in Great Britain by
Hartnolls Limited, Bodmin, Cornwall

A CIP catalogue record for this book
is available from the British Library

To Jill Hutchinson, my sister

With acknowledgements to Steve Bennett,
Gary Kitchen and Roy Lewis
of the Devon and Cornwall Police

1

'Shall I get you something?'

'Like what?'

'I don't know, Ian. Don't snap. A brandy, or lemonade, I've heard that's good for sea-sickness.' Moira was becoming increasingly irritated with her husband's mood.

Ian's brain told him a brandy seemed like a good idea but his stomach told him otherwise. 'I am *not* sea-sick. It was probably those sodding mussels last night.'

'I had them too,' Moira pointed out sweetly.

At that moment he felt he almost hated her. She stood serenely in front of his chair, which was fortunately bolted to the deck; at forty, she remained slim and pretty, her soft fair hair resting on her shoulders, her cheeks glowing from a walk around the upper deck. The whole reason for the trip had been a belated celebration of her fortieth birthday which, in itself, made him feel old.

The weather was not particularly rough – he could have coped with that better; it was just the way in which the ship was pitching and rolling relentlessly which did not agree with him. When he tried to walk, his feet refused to obey messages from his central nervous system and the croissant which, smothered in butter and jam, he had dunked in his coffee at breakfast was something best not remembered.

'We'll be back soon. You'll be fine once we're on dry land.' But Ian Roper vowed he would never, ever cross the Channel by boat again as long as he lived. Not that he'd be going through the tunnel either; the idea of it was worse than that of being stuck in a lift. Looking back, there were few good points about the holiday to compensate for the awful crossing. Moira liked a warm climate with some culture thrown in; Greece and Italy for preference. He would have been just as happy staying in England, seeing the countryside, watching a bit of football and sampling various real ales. France had been the compromise except that as it was November there was no sun, and he had had to make do with wine because there was no decent beer – what's more, he couldn't speak the lingo and Moira had shown him up by being able to make herself understood in schoolgirl French. And if Detective bloody Sergeant Barry Swan had not decided to get married and everyone else had not had the foresight to book their leave early, they could have gone in June.

An undue amount of time had been spent bickering. All right, he had to accept it was mostly his fault and when Moira accused him of acting like a spoilt child he did try to make an effort. But, to be fair, she had been distant at times, wrapped up in her own thoughts, and now it was all over she was smiling, glad to be going home, and that was not like her.

She remained standing in front of him, an expression of martyred patience on her face, but he could not think of one civil thing to say. How could he when they were lurching about in the miserable, grey sea, the engines throbbing beneath him?

It was Moira who drove the car off the ferry and home. Ian sat in the passenger seat with his arms folded and his lips pressed firmly together. He was, as she had said he would, feeling better, but there was no way he was going to admit it.

It always came as a surprise that after an absence of any length of time 14 Belmont Terrace looked no different from when they had left it. Ian picked up the torch he had left in readiness inside the front door and switched on the electricity at the mains. On the doormat was a stack of post, most of it, judging by the envelopes, the usual assortment of junk mail.

'It's freezing in here. Reset the heating, would you, while I

6

see to this lot?' Moira indicated the suitcases at her feet. 'Then,' she added, smiling, 'I'll treat you to a curry.'

'Great. I've been looking forward to that for the past week. And a couple of pints of Adnams first.'

Moira nodded but refrained from pointing out that one did not usually recover from food poisoning that rapidly.

'Welcome back, sir. Good holiday?' One by one those on duty at Rickenham Green headquarters learned that Detective Chief Inspector Roper was back from leave. He was pleased to be back; it showed on his face and in the way he took the stairs to his office two at a time. All the walking Moira had insisted on had improved his fitness. Telephones rang, computer console keys clicked softly, and men and women, uniformed or otherwise, moved swiftly from one part of the building to another. Yes, it was good to be back.

He reported to Superintendent Thorne, who made polite inquiries about France. Now it was behind him, Ian realised he had enjoyed it more than he believed at the time.

'I don't think you'll find any major problems,' Thorne told him in his Birmingham accent. 'DS Swan's done a good job. You ought to talk him into going for his inspector's exams.'

He might have been dead, not on leave, Ian thought when he saw his clear desktop, the in-tray almost empty, the out-tray completely so. DS Swan had, indeed, been doing a good job. Momentarily he felt superfluous. There was only one way to cure that, a mug of canteen coffee. It was guaranteed to take your mind off anything.

As the day progressed and reports and memos were placed in front of him, several concerning cases he was not yet familiar with, he began to get back into the rhythm of work. Life was reverting to normal. At five thirty, when DCs Emmanuel and Campbell asked if he was going to join them for a pint in the Feathers, the reversion was complete.

*

It was unnervingly quiet, almost ominously so. The weeks leading up to Christmas usually involved the added burden of increased petty crime, but this year the figures hardly altered. No one remarked upon it, no one dared. They kept their files up to date and their mouths shut because it was tempting fate to mention their good luck. No one wanted leave or a day off to be cancelled. It was bad enough having to work normal duties over the Christmas period without overtime, worse when there were a wife and mother-in-law to berate you for not being there to watch the children open their presents. There were exceptions; the ones with no one at home would have welcomed extra hours.

Operation Keyring, activated a year ago, had helped reduce thefts both from and of cars. Car-parks were better lit, with tighter security, and most of them had emergency telephones on each level. There were also pre-Christmas reminders in the weekly *Rickenham Herald* not to leave goods visible on the back seat. Even so, there were a few incidents, and there were still people foolish enough to leave signs that their house was temporarily uninhabited.

Hardly anyone bothered to comment about the good old days when doors were never locked and keys hung from string through the letter-box. The world has changed, Sergeant Baker thought as he completed the forms relating to a young mother whose children's clothes had been stolen from a line hanging in her garage, and the people in it have changed, and if you can't accept it, you go mad. He smiled kindly at the young woman, feeling sorry for her. She did not look as if she had much and he did not have the heart to tell her it was unlikely she would ever see the things again.

And then it was over. Christmas and the New Year had come and gone. One or two officers had swapped shifts to fit in with family celebrations but no one had missed any time off. There was, as always, a seasonal spate of 'domestics': husbands and wives, too closely confined for too long, arguing over who had or had not done what and ending up battering each other. Matters were often brought to a head by a houseful of relatives who did not particularly like each other and who had little contact during the other fifty weeks of the year yet fooled themselves into thinking that because it was Christmas they would be infected with a dose of goodwill. Presents were broken and children cried, adults over-ate and drank too much – none of which, Ian knew, made for a happy household. He thanked a God he was not sure he believed in that he had been delivered from all that. He and Moira were only children, Moira's mother the only surviving parent, and she took herself off on a cruise each year. There was only Mark, eighteen now and away at college; having spent Christmas at home, he apologetically explained that he had arranged to spend the New Year in Devon with friends. Ian had looked at his son and had known that he was suddenly a man, free, legally and morally, to make his own decisions about how and where he spent his time. His bone structure and colouring were Moira's, his height he inherited from Ian, but where he had acquired his artistic talent remained a mystery.

Ian's one concession to the festive season had been to take Moira to the annual divisional bash: she always enjoyed it, and it did no harm for a DCI to be seen socialising. The only people from work with whom they mixed were Barry and Lucy Swan, Judy Robbins and Doc Harris, but he wasn't strictly police.

Moira worked for a firm of builders but it was too small to have an organised celebration. They compromised by keeping it to staff only and having a few drinks followed by a meal in the Greek restaurant. Ian would have hated it; he cringed when she related the plate-smashing ritual and their hilarious attempts at the national dances.

On New Year's Eve they went to the Harrises'. There were just the four of them, Ian and Moira and the Doc and Shirley. The Doc, as he was known to everyone, including his wife, was a GP and one of the police surgeons as well as being an old friend. The next morning both men looked as bad as they felt but received no sympathy from their respective wives.

Ian went back to work on the 2nd. 'Is that it?' He was

9

scanning the list of activities for the night of the 31st. A few broken windows, a few broken heads, but nothing out of the ordinary.

DS Barry Swan hung up his coat. 'And a happy New Year to you, too.'

'Yeah. Sorry. Have a good time?'

'Quiet, but very enjoyable.' Barry, whose reputation as a womaniser had faded since his relationship with Lucy had begun, was not about to admit that he had more than enjoyed the gracious elegance of Lucy's parents' country home and the genteel manner of living which was carried on within it. He had to retain some remnants of his image.

'Thank God it's all over. I hear the Tucker boy's out.'

Barry groaned. 'Great. We'll need a permanent patrol car out at Frampton in that case. I thought he got eighteen months.'

'Served some of it on remand and got a reduced sentence for being a good boy. Why is it they can behave inside but the minute they're released ... oh, forget it.' It was an age-old argument Ian had with himself.

Moira's one concession to Christmas had been to decorate the small silver tree which was folded away in the attic the rest of the year. She had done it for Mark's sake. When Ian returned home that night it was nowhere to be seen. Neither was his wife. She seemed to be out a lot lately.

A fortnight later, on a bitterly cold day, Ian stood in front of the wash-basin in the gents' toilets and pulled down the lower lid of his right eye to examine the white. One of the best pleasures in life was a few pints of Adnams beer but he wondered if he had been overdoing it. Satisfied there was nothing to see but a few healthy red veins, he took his comb from his jacket pocket and ran it through his thick hair, now greying at the sides. He had to stoop as the mirror was set at a height for men of average dimensions, not those who were six feet four inches. He threw back his shoulders and sucked in his stomach. Not bad for his age, he decided, but did Moira still think so? There was no time to ponder this question because, reflected in the mirror, he saw the worried face of a uniformed officer.

'White, female, probably mid-twenties. Cause of death, according to the para-medics, strangulation. That's as much as I know,' Barry told Ian as they hurried across the car-park. It was dark. The easterly wind, sweeping across the flat countryside from the sea, caught at Barry's raincoat, filling it so that it billowed out around him, and ruffled his pale hair where it grew slightly long over his collar, playing with the bits brushed back over his crown to disguise the thinness there. He opened the car door, holding the handle to prevent it swinging back, then got into the driving seat. He enjoyed driving and Ian never objected as he was content to be a passenger.

'Where're we going?'

'Alexander Road. Just off Saxborough Road.'

'I know where it is, Barry. Quietish street, private houses. It's not a problem area.'

They did not converse much on the ten-minute drive: the traffic was heavy and their minds were already ahead of them, anticipating what they might find. Strangulation, or asphyxiation – at least there would not be any blood.

The road was not dissimilar to Belmont Terrace where Ian lived. The houses were brick-built, solid-looking, but nothing out of the ordinary. Cars were parked down both sides but there were still plenty of spaces. Soon, when the rest of the team arrived, they would be taken. There were low brick walls dividing the small front gardens from the pavement. Behind them, one or two residents had planted privet or box. Second homes, Ian guessed, three-bedroom: the type chosen after a flat was outgrown and a family had been started, the second rung up the property ladder, except that he and Moira had not taken a third step.

The arrival of the ambulance followed by that of a patrol car had brought several neighbours out on to their respective

11

doorsteps where they now stood, cardigans or coats hugged close to their bodies in the chill evening air as they awaited developments.

The small gate belonging to number 16 was neatly closed despite the presence of a uniformed officer at the door. Ian took the four steps necessary to reach that door. Barry followed, closing the gate behind him. It was as if, flimsy though this structure was, it still served as a barrier between the tragedy inside the house and the prurient curiosity of the neighbours.

PC Jeffries saluted and informed Ian that PC Freeman was inside, in the kitchen with the husband. The body was in the living-room and no one, apart from the para-medics who were first on the scene after the husband, had entered or left the house.

'Good,' Ian said. 'Carry on here.' PC Jeffries was now responsible for recording the comings and goings of every person, no matter what their rank or status, who had anything to do with the case.

The hallway was not very wide but it was cheerful. The walls were palest pink; framed charcoal sketches hung at intervals and continued on up the stairs. The carpet was a warm red; this, too, continued up the stairs and also into the living-room and a second room behind it. It would not, however, be stained with a darker red.

'In there, sir.'

Ian nudged open the nearest door with his elbow although it was probably too late for any decent prints as the husband had allegedly discovered the body and the ambulance crew had followed him.

Debbie Orchard lay on the floor. At first glance she might have been asleep. She was wearing a jogging suit and trainers, none of which appeared to have been disturbed. Her hair was brown, cut short to frame her face. Ian bent down, resting his hands on his thighs to steady himself. Even allowing for changes which a violent death had made to her features it

12

seemed unlikely that Debbie had been more than averagely good-looking. Pleasant-faced, maybe, but certainly no beauty. One quick glance was enough. Barry nodded his own recognition. The pin-point haemorrhages in her eyes spoke for themselves. Debbie Orchard had been strangled. It was, of course, up to the police surgeon to pronounce her dead and the Home Office pathologist or the post-mortem to show the cause of death. They were formalities in this case. No suspicious death this, it was unquestionably murder. There was little they could do, it was up to the experts now. They would take a swift look around, disturbing nothing, then speak to the husband.

'Nice place,' Barry said quietly. 'And very clean.' It was so clean that Forensic might have a good chance of finding something. If Debbie or her husband had recently dusted and vacuumed the carpets any traces picked up now might well belong to the murderer.

The living-room was an apt description of where the body lay. The settee and chairs were soft and looked comfortable. It was warm, centrally heated, and there was a bookcase taking up most of one wall, into which had been fitted a television set. But it was small, a twelve-inch screen, and in such a place that it was obviously not a priority in the Orchards' lives.

The room behind was a shambles by comparison. Equally comfortable, it held more bookshelves, a desk upon which rested a computer and a couple of chairs, but there were textbooks and papers everywhere. It was some sort of study.

Upstairs was a bathroom and the bedrooms – all, viewed from each doorway, tidy. There were no signs of forced entry. The motive did not appear to be sexual or robbery.

'The husband now?'

'Yes. The husband now,' Ian replied grimly. No forced entry, no disturbance, nothing taken – it pointed, as was so often the case, to the next-of-kin or someone who knew the victim well. And yet it was too tidy; surely some effort would have been made to at least make it appear like a robbery. It was still beyond Ian's comprehension that spouses were murdered when divorce was so simple. But life, of course, was not that simple.

They both blinked when they entered the kitchen. It was much larger than they expected as an extension had been built out into the garden; compared with the rest of the house, which was warmly, but dimly, lit, here was an oasis of brightness. Stainless steel gleamed under the harsh fluorescent tubes and white appliances reflected the light. Around a glass table were four chrome chairs. In one of these sat Roy Orchard, his elbows on the table, his head between his hands. Beside him was a mug of tea, untouched and no longer warm.

Ian introduced himself and Barry but was unsure whether Orchard had heard because he made no response for several seconds. 'Why her?' he asked when he finally looked up. 'Why my Debbie?'

Roy Orchard, his features distorted with grief, was still an extremely handsome man. Ian had no answer to give him. Hating himself for having to do so, he resorted to the platitudes which would lead to an opening for his questions. He doubted if the words existed which would lessen the pain of the bereaved.

'Mr Orchard,' he began, 'there is nothing I can say to restore your wife's life to her, but we shall do everything within our power to find the person responsible for taking it.' Orchard looked at him blankly and nodded. 'We need to know what happened today, and we need to know about Debbie. Are you up to answering a few questions?'

The expression on Orchard's face showed that he thought he might be under suspicion. With a great effort he pulled himself upright, brushed back a lock of almost black hair and interlaced his fingers before placing his hands on the table, where he seemed to have more control over them.

'If you prefer,' Ian continued, 'you could just tell us what happened today. From the time you got up.'

He sighed. 'All right. I know it has to be done.' He paused;

the morning seemed light years away after all the things that had happened. 'It was the same as any other day. We got up at seven thirty, we always do on schooldays. Debbie first, she's never minded the dark mornings, she made toast and coffee while I used the bathroom. Then I washed up while she got ready. We left for school at twenty past eight.'

'School?'

'Yes. Oh, I see. We're both teachers at the comprehensive.'

'And you both went together?'

'We've only got one car. We agreed it's an extravagance to have two, and Debbie's keen on protecting the environment. Not a fanatic, you understand, but she likes to do her bit. Our friends can't understand how we can live and work together but it isn't like that, we hardly see each other during the day.' He was still referring to his wife in the present tense; the fact of her death had not yet registered. As far as Ian was concerned it was a good thing. Once numbness took over it was difficult to get witnesses to talk.

'And today? Did you see Debbie at school?'

'No. I parked and we walked a few yards together but my classes are all in the main building, Debbie's are either outside or in the gym or the shower block.' Which explained the jogging suit. Debbie Orchard had taught PE, or sports or games or whatever fancy name they called it these days. 'At lunchtime I had a department meeting and on Wednesdays Debbie doesn't have any classes after two thirty so she leaves early.'

'How does she get home?'

'How? In the car. She usually does the shopping on the way.'

'And how do you get home, Mr Orchard?' The comprehensive school was some distance away.

'I walk. I need the exercise. If the weather's really foul I catch a bus.'

'And today?'

There was the slightest hesitation. 'I walked.'

15

'Who would know your wife leaves early on Wednesdays?'

'Almost anyone at school, I would imagine, and some of her friends.'

Barry was about to speak. Ian gave a barely perceptible shake of the head. This must not sound like an interrogation. 'Is it usual to hold meetings in the lunch hour?'

'Not really. This one had been postponed several times due to various commitments – it was convenient, that's all.'

It would be checked but Ian knew it was pointless to lie about something so easily verifiable. And it should not prove difficult to discover exactly what time Debbie Orchard had left the school premises. An overwhelming thought crossed Ian's mind. There were approximately thirteen hundred pupils at the school, plus numerous staff. Was it possible one of them had killed her? A boy, because of some silly crush, say? Or more than a crush. Eighteen-year-olds, as he well knew, were men these days – it might even have been a full-blown affair.

'Has anything unusual happened lately? Telephone calls, callers, anything at school?'

Roy Orchard closed his eyes. 'No, nothing,' he finally said.

'And your wife wasn't expecting any visitors today?'

He shook his head. 'And she didn't have any enemies. If you knew Debbie you'd understand that. Everybody liked her. Everybody.' He did not see the inconsistency in the remark. It was plain one person did not.

Beside the fridge were two Safeway carrier bags, still bulging. Orchard saw the direction of Ian's gaze. 'She didn't even have time to put the groceries away.' Only then did tears fill his eyes as he realised the food the bags contained would not be cooked by his wife.

'May I?' Ian reached into the nearest carrier and, from between a jar of coffee and a cellophane wrapper containing three different coloured peppers, withdrew the till receipt which he had noticed. It was dated that day. For once he was up on the medics. It was timed at 15.02. Debbie could not have been killed before, say, three thirty. 'I know how hard this is for you. Just one more question then we'll leave it for this evening. You rang us at ten past five – '

Roy's head shot up. 'I know what you think – you think I killed her, don't you? God, how could you? I loved her. I'm sorry, I can't take any of this in properly. I didn't do it and there's no mystery as to where I was. I do an hour of private English coaching on Wednesdays. Jennifer Knowles. She lives in the next street. Number 34. I left there just after five.'

'Thank you, Mr Orchard. I'm sorry this has been so stressful. There will be other men here soon – is there somewhere you can stay tonight? We can arrange transport for you.'

'I'll go to my mother's. I . . . when . . .?' He waved a hand which Ian took to mean he was indicating the room where his wife lay.

'Not for some time. It really will be better for you to go to your mother's.'

There were more of the team present now. Ian had heard John Cotton's voice faintly through the closed door. He was head of Scene of Crime. Doc Harris would be out there, and the photographers, and it would not be a pleasant experience for Roy Orchard to see what they had to do or know that drawers and cupboards were being opened and searched, their personal lives delved into and pored over by complete strangers as if they were of no consequence. It was a total invasion of privacy but one which had to take place.

'Would you like someone to accompany you? It's easier sometimes to break the news with a bit of support.'

Roy said he would and gave them his parents' address. It also saved them from having to explain that he couldn't take the car. Forensic would want to go over that, too, in case Debbie had given her killer a lift. Once he was off the premises Ian and Barry went to speak to whoever was in the living-room. Harry Ford, the Home Office pathologist, arrived, fairly quickly for him as he had vast distances to cover. 'I hardly think my services were required here,' he said sardonically, 'but as we all know, rules are rules. If you want my opinion the PM won't show any more than I can tell you right now.'

17

'An opinion, Harry? What's this, a New Year's resolution?'

'Very droll. She's been strangled; Forensic haven't finished so I can't check yet for sexual assault, but it seems unlikely unless he stayed to dress her carefully. You've lost a bit of weight, haven't you?'

Ian was gratified. The five pounds he shed whilst on holiday had remained off. They chatted for only a few minutes before leaving. They had already arranged for a squad to start on house-to-house inquiries. 'Look at them,' Ian said as they walked to the car. 'Like bloody vultures.' More people had gathered with the arrival of more vehicles. He despised them.

Back at headquarters DCI Roper ensured that the control room was operational. Although the interview with Roy Orchard had not been particularly illuminating, it was surprising how much they already knew about the victim. Debbie Orchard was twenty-nine, older than she looked, of average weight, height and appearance. She was a schoolteacher, her hair cut in a fashion suitable for windy hockey fields, tennis in the summer and endless showers. She took a pride in her home, which was tastefully decorated and extremely clean. From the contents of her shopping bags it seemed she preferred to cook from scratch rather than use packets or frozen food. The house was full of books which suggested she had an inquiring mind and, as there was only the one small television, a preference for more intellectual pursuits. Given time Ian would know as much about this stranger as he did about his wife. Which reminded him, he had better telephone Moira. It was a rare occasion when he forgot to let her know he was going to be late. Some of them did not bother, he knew that, they just took it as their right to go home whenever they chose, their wives and girlfriends worried or frustrated or furious whilst they had a few beers after work.

'Will it be on the local news later?' Moira asked when he told her.

'I expect so. The basics anyway. I'm just on my way to see the Super. We'll need to make sure all the relatives are informed first.'

Moira knew better than to ask the name; Ian would tell her in his own time. 'What about food? Will you have eaten?'

He glanced at his watch. It was nearly nine already and there was at least another hour's work before he could be satisfied that the framework within which such an investigation operated was firmly in place. Then there might be time to call in at the Crown, where the landlord wouldn't rush him if he wanted the second pint. 'Just leave something handy I can make into a sandwich. There's no need to wait up if you're tired.' But he was sure she would, Moira always did at such times or if he was under a lot of stress; he appreciated her concern and her sound common sense, but mostly he simply appreciated her presence.

At eleven forty-five, having had time for those two pints, Ian put his key in the lock and stepped into the warmth of 14 Belmont Terrace. It had felt like home since the first day they moved in. He pushed down the snib and slid the chain across then opened the sitting-room door. Only the small table lamp was on and there were no books or papers lying around. Throwing his jacket over the back of an armchair he went to see if Moira was in the kitchen. It was in darkness. Flicking on the switch he saw the sandwich on the worktop, carefully wrapped in film; a mug containing a tea-bag stood next to the kettle. Was she out again? Ian felt a twinge of uncertainty. The upstairs hall light was on. He mounted the stairs and quietly opened their bedroom door. Moira was in bed but his sense of relief was short-lived.

'Hello, ' she said, 'I didn't hear you come in.'

Ian swallowed. Sitting up in bed with a book in her hands, Moira could have passed for twenty-five. Her hair shone as she had washed it that evening and her skin, in the glow of the bedside light, was as silky as the material of her nightdress.

As soon as the words were out of his mouth he hated himself for uttering them. 'I thought you might have waited up tonight, knowing what's going on.'

Moira's smile vanished. 'You did say not to if I was tired.'

19

'You're wide awake.'

She bit her lip. Not tonight, she thought, I know what he's like when there's a big case on. 'I'm sorry,' she said, but for what she wasn't sure.

'It's all right.' Ian came to the side of the bed and kissed her on the forehead. 'I'll just have that sandwich and a shot of something then I'll be up.'

The door rattled as he closed it because his hand was shaking. He was in his fifties; Moira was only forty, and an exceptionally attractive woman. He was irritable and untidy and sometimes took her for granted and now, with Mark at college and her full-time job in the office at the builders, she was independent. There would be many men in her life now, younger, fitter men, men with charm and jokes to offer her. Was that the reason why she was out so frequently – had she met someone else? With difficulty he made himself stop thinking about it. Moira had never given him any cause to doubt her feelings. Until now. The phrase sprang unbidden into his mind. And when the holiday was over she had seemed so glad to be coming home instead of making her usual remarks about being sorry it had to end. It was ridiculous – the one thing he constantly said at work was, if in doubt ask, but he was unable to do so. He was terrified of receiving the wrong answer.

Moira was asleep when he got into bed an hour later. He put his arm around her and pulled her tightly to him; she muttered something but did not wake. Surprisingly, sleep came easily to him.

2

Whilst the house-to-house inquiries continued Ian arranged for the members of staff at the comprehensive school to be interviewed. Staff-room gossip might hold a clue. If the atmosphere of that large organisation was anything like the station house, an affair or any disruption between Debbie Orchard and a pupil was sure to be known.

It was quiet at the mortuary so the post-mortem was fixed for later that afternoon. DCI Roper and DS Swan were expected to attend. Doc Harris, if he was available, usually turned up to watch although it was not part of his duties. His wife Shirley had told him often enough the world was a better place for old-fashioned GPs like himself, men who had time to listen and reassure rather than hand out a prescription, but Doc Harris was a frustrated pathologist. He was not able to attend that Thursday.

'We didn't learn anything there we didn't already know,' Barry said when they left. Debbie had been fit, which, from her job, was to be expected. She appeared to have no illness at the time of her death; there were no healed fractures, no distinguishing marks and only two small areas of scar tissue from injuries acquired many years ago. She had neither borne a child nor been pregnant; the stomach contents had been digested, which confirmed the likelihood that her last meal had been consumed at school.

By the time they returned to the station it was raining and the reception area was wet with dirty footprints. There were reports to be read, those from the house-to-house inquiries and others from the school. House-to-house first, Ian decided, as these were the people who might have actually witnessed something as opposed to the background information and hearsay from other teachers. But he knew that if anything relevant had come up someone would have told him.

Only one neighbour, a Mrs Biddick, was able to help. She had been leaving her house to go to the corner shop when she saw Debbie Orchard pull in and get out of the car. They had waved to each other. 'Yes, she was alone,' Mrs Biddick said. 'It must've been getting on for four because when I got to the shop there was a crowd of schoolkids ahead of me buying sweets and that.' But she had not seen anyone enter or leave 16 Alexander Road. Neither had anyone else.

'I suppose it isn't that surprising at that time of day,' Ian said. 'People are either at work or collecting children from school and maybe doing a bit of shopping on the way home, and if the killer turned up at, say, just before five, it would have been dark and a lot of women would be in the kitchen preparing a meal.'

'It's quite a busy road, too,' Barry added. 'A lot of people park there to use the shops at the top because it saves coming into the town centre. If he was driving, one more vehicle wouldn't stand out.'

The map pinned to the wall showed several rows of houses, their gardens back to back with an access lane separating them. At the eastern end of Alexander Road was a sub-post office which also sold newspapers, tobacco and basic groceries. Next to it was a video hire place which meant traffic was coming and going until nine thirty at night. The Orchards did not patronise the latter and rarely used the former except to pay for their paper bill once a month. They, like many others, enjoyed the luxury of having the paper delivered so it could be read over breakfast without their having to get dressed to go and buy it.

Detective Constable Campbell tapped at the door, which was partly open. 'We thought you'd want to know right away, sir. We found this at the house. It's a bit mucky, it was in the

22

pedal bin.' He handed over a transparent cover which held no more than a two-inch square of paper. It had been screwed up but was now flattened. It was a bus ticket obtained from one of the Rickenham Runabout buses, a privately operated company whose small, single-decker transport circulated the town and took in routes Eastern National missed. The information printed on it told them that an adult fare of forty-two pence had been paid. The route was 27, from stop 11 to stop 6. But what was interesting was that it bore the previous day's date and a boarding time of 15.37.

Ian nodded his comprehension of what it might mean. 'So Orchard's lying. Now I wonder why that might be. Have you checked with the bus company, Alan?'

Predictably, DC Campbell said he had. 'Stop 11 is directly outside the school, 6 is at the end of Saxborough Road, the wrong end for Alexander Road. It doesn't mean he got off there, though, once you've got a ticket there's no one to check them. And there's nothing there, houses mostly and one pub which keeps to the old opening hours.'

'Thanks. Well done.'

'Oh, and the journey, on average, takes seven minutes.'

DCI Roper suppressed a grin. Alan Campbell was meticulous in his work but he was also a pedant; he had probably already sent someone to make that same journey, which was the next thing Ian was going to suggest. He had, indeed, done so. It was important: it might have given Orchard enough time to strangle his wife.

'It doesn't make sense. Mrs Knowles confirmed Orchard arrived on time for her daughter's lesson and that he left when he said he did.' Barry picked up the relevant notes to double check. Both Jennifer and her mother agreed on the time. It was just before four o'clock, Roy was always punctual. He had left at five-past five, refusing the offer of a cup of tea. Jennifer had been doing well under his auspices and had been in tears when she was interviewed. It crossed the mind of the WPC who was questioning her whether there was more to it than a pupil/teacher relationship, but after assessing the fourteen-

23

year-old carefully she decided against it. Jennifer was over-weight, remarkably plain and immature for her age.

'Find anything?'

Barry slid the file over. 'Nope. Look, if he normally leaves school on Wednesdays immediately classes are over at three thirty that gives him just enough time to get to the Knowles' place on foot. If he's delayed he can fall back on the bus, there're plenty at that time of day. Fine. But why lie about it? And why get off at the wrong end of Saxborough Road?'

'Beats me, Barry, especially as he was still on time and, according to Campbell, it takes six or seven minutes to walk to the Knowles'.'

'Which leaves approximately five minutes for him to have nipped home for a spot of murder before calmly helping Jennifer analyse Shakespeare or whatever.'

'Stranger things have occurred. Come on, there's only one way to find out. We'll ask.' Immediately, and seemingly unconnectedly, Ian wondered exactly where Moira was at that moment.

'She *was* interviewed, along with the others. I remember the name.'

'Perhaps she didn't mention it because she thought it had no bearing on the case.'

'Come off it, Barry. The wife of a man she is more than interested in is murdered and this woman believes we're not going to find out she's panting with lust for him?'

'Orchard didn't see any reason to mention it himself, nor, if you recall, did any of the other staff.'

'But if she's as besotted as he claims . . .' Ian left the sentence unfinished. He could not think of a single case of one woman strangling another – smothering, maybe – and he did not seriously consider she had got someone else to do the job, although that wouldn't be a first.

Ian contacted headquarters via the car radio and asked for Elizabeth Sandra Jones to be picked up and brought in. Liza, as she was generally known, had been questioned in the relative comfort of the staff-room, but there would be no such niceties on this occasion. She had been less than honest about her dealings with the Orchards, and she was not about to have the advantage of her own territory.

Liza Jones arrived fifteen minutes after Ian and Barry got back and was kept waiting for a further quarter of an hour.

'Miss Jones, I expect you've guessed why we want to talk to you again,' Ian began.

'It's Ms.'

He groaned inwardly. He detested the appellation as much as he hated having to pronounce it. 'All right, Ms Jones then. We happen to know you received a letter from Mr Orchard some time yesterday afternoon. Do you have it with you?'

'How did you . . .' Her face reddened and she bit her bottom lip as if to physically prevent herself saying something she shouldn't. 'Did he tell you that?'

Neither man answered her. Instead Barry said, 'Why didn't you tell us how you felt about Mr Orchard? It would have saved you this embarrassment.'

'Because it was nothing to do with Debbie.'

'Nothing to do with Debbie? Really, *Ms* Jones' – Ian's sarcasm wasn't wasted – 'I'm not inclined to agree with you. I think the fact that you were chasing her husband has everything to do with her.'

'No. You don't understand. I know she's dead but she wasn't good enough for him. I can't help it if I didn't like her. She was too quiet, too concerned about things, and Roy could have done much better for himself in the looks department.'

'Meaning what? Like yourself?'

'Pardon?'

'You heard me. Was that it, was that why you went round there yesterday afternoon, to make sure you had him to yourself?'

Liza Jones looked terrified but Ian had only been trying to shock her into further admissions. She was one of those

25

women who aptly fit the description of doll-like. Her hair was naturally blonde and the blue eyes and pretty face belied her calculating, vindictive nature. But more than that, she was petite. It was virtually impossible for her to have over-powered, let alone strangled, Debbie Orchard.

Liza looked up with renewed hope in her face. Debbie was dead, she had a serious chance with Roy now if she bided her time. 'Roy can't deny he was interested, whatever he told you. Women can sense these things. It was just that he didn't want me to get the sack. The school does not approve of such relationships.'

'Neither do I,' Ian informed her. This time she did not blush. 'And according to Mr Orchard there was no relationship.'

'No. Well, there would have been, sooner or later.'

There was no way of disproving this but both Ian and Barry felt otherwise. Orchard's story had the ring of truth. He had explained that Liza had made her intentions clear and although he had rejected them she was beginning to make a nuisance of herself. Other members of staff had noticed and he had to put an end to it. 'She started ringing me at home on the most feeble pretences,' Roy said. 'I told Debbie what was going on, I had to, for both our sakes. It would've been awful if she heard it from someone else. I had to make her under-stand there was nothing in it, that it was her I loved. I wrote to Liza, written words often have more power than the spoken ones. I told her this nonsense had to stop and that if it didn't I would go to the headmaster.' And, very sensibly, he had kept a copy of the letter, which was now in Ian's pocket in case he needed to produce it.

Roy Orchard's reasons for lying might have been stupid but they seemed justifiable to him. He had written that letter while his class were making notes on a text he had asked them to study, and he wanted to deliver it immediately, not trust it to the post and have to get through another day without Liza knowing he had had enough. Her house was on the bus route home and there was no danger of her seeing him because she ran the drama club on Wednesdays. When he found Debbie he knew he had to protect her memory, '. . . and,' he candidly admitted, 'my own reputation. Nor did I want to make trouble for Liza if it could be avoided. You see, I thought if it came out people would always believe there really had been something in it, they always prefer to think the worst. How could I live if Debbie's friends and family thought I was being unfaithful to her, that I was in the wrong, and she is the one who gets murdered? I thought you might think I killed her myself, to be with Liza.'

Ian pulled out the copy of the letter and unfolded it, allowing Ms Jones enough of a glimpse to see what it was. She bowed her head, humiliated that these men were aware of its contents. She saw she had no option but to confirm Roy's story.

'You may go now,' Ian said, 'but please bear in mind that wasting the time and resources of the police is frowned upon.' She was not offered transport home.

It was a little after seven thirty and there seemed no point in staying later. The background information was building up but there was still nothing concrete to work with. The Orchards' financial status appeared to be secure and Debbie's husband had said, 'Chocolate, that was what she called her only vice. She had to ration herself to a small piece each day.' But they would check. They had to.

'Come on, you can buy me a pint.'

'Forgive me for pointing this out, but I rather think it's your turn,' Barry replied.

They did not stay long because they were both driving. Beer, Ian supposed, was his vice, but he, too, rationed himself when he had to. The wind had dropped and a clear, high sky glittered with stars. He picked out the Plough and what he thought might be Orion's Belt, but he wasn't certain, that was as far as his astronomical knowledge went. After the warmth of the Crown he thought it might be freezing but the grass on the Green was damp underfoot and blackish under the street lights. The windscreen of his car was clear, if a little dirty.

From around the corner smells of Chinese cooking wafted from the extractor fan at the back of the take-away. His stomach rumbled and he hoped it was not to be a low-calorie night at home.

'I shall be out tomorrow night,' Moira informed him as she dished up something which she said was a cheaper version of cassoulet but which looked like sausage stew to Ian. It steamed on the plate and he breathed in garlic before being surprised at how tasty it was with the chick peas and tomatoes. On top was crusty bread with melted cheese and there was a glass of average red wine to go with it.

'Not bad, considering it's French.' He was reminded again of the unsuccessful holiday, of his suspicions – and now Moira was going out again the following night.

'I'm glad you like it because there's enough for tomorrow.'

'Are you going anywhere nice?' He jabbed his fork into a chunk of sausage and avoided her eyes.

'Just for a drink. I won't be late.'

It was an evasive answer but he did not press her. He watched as Moira neatly finished her meal then cleared the table. She was not acting suspiciously, or nervously – if he was honest, she seemed no different at all. Yet the uncertainty continued to nag at him, making him edgy. In bed he flung an arm across her in his usual way and tried to forget his worries.

He had executed the perfect crime. They could search but there would be no fingerprints, no nothing. He had worn gloves, a hat pulled well down and anti-static clothing. And he and the woman had no connection. People were such fools, volunteering information to strangers, so many of them did it, which made his plans so much easier. And when the job was finally completed, if – which he doubted – anyone questioned him, he had proof he was not involved. He would also have a perfect alibi.

He was a good-looking man, his body nicely proportioned,

but when he smiled it was a leer, the malevolence of his nature undeniable.

The more Ian studied Roy Orchard's movements on the day his wife was murdered, the more convinced he became that he was not the man they were seeking. The investigation was widening from family, close friends and workmates to acquaintances and anyone else with whom Debbie might have come into contact. Soon they would have to begin on the pupils.

So far Roy's assessment that his wife was liked and respected was, apart from the exception of Liza Jones, corroborated. Teaching staff said she had taken a great deal of interest in her students and was always willing to take part in after-school activities and matches, even on Saturdays, often travelling to other schools with a team. Her interests were reading, gardening and sewing but she did not belong to any clubs: the days of the extra-curricular matches varied, and to join something on a regular basis was impractical. Her parents were dead, wiped out in a car accident when she was ten. It was an aunt who had brought her up along with her own three children. Unlikely as it seemed, the deeper they dug into her past the less reason they found for anyone wishing her dead. A total stranger had not been ruled out, but how and why would she have let him into her home? And what was the motive if not sexual or for financial gain? No builders or tradesmen had called for at least a year and no matter how hard they tried they found nothing to fit the hypothetical supposition that it was Debbie, not Roy, who had a lover.

Results from the lab at Huntingdon filtered in. Carpet sweepings contained grit which corresponded to that from the mess the workmen at the end of the road had left when they replaced some gas pipes. These men had been traced and questioned. The name Debbie Orchard meant nothing to them, nor did the photograph they were shown. The job had been completed three days before her death. There were hairs and fibres; the hairs matched those of the Orchards, the fibres might prove useful later, but only if they had a suspect. By the weekend there were five operational squads flat out following their own routes and still there was nothing. 'It's like pissing into the wind,' Barry said when they packed up at lunchtime on Saturday. He was not renowned for a poetic turn of phrase but Ian had to agree with him.

Leaving the building and realising that despite the blustery wind it was quite mild, Ian toyed with the idea of going to watch Norwich play. They were at home that week and he'd missed the previous two games, but he was more concerned about his relationship with Moira: and those who knew him well would guess the depth of his concern if he willingly missed a football match.

'I thought you'd go straight to the game,' she said when he found her in the kitchen ironing. 'They're at home, aren't they?'

He was hurt. Did she not see the effort he was making? He had expected her to be pleased but it seemed as if she was treating his presence as one which would merely be in the way when she wanted to do the housework. The clock on the cooker told him he still had time to get there for the kick-off. There was a pain inside him that was physical as he drove out of the town. For his own peace of mind he had to confront her – not tonight though, because they had arranged to meet Barry and Lucy Swan at seven thirty and he did not want to go out if there was an atmosphere between them. They were having a few drinks and a meal, a curry, he supposed, because the couple of drinks often turned into more by which time it was too late to go anywhere other than an Indian restaurant.

Moira was in the shower when he returned. When she had finished he stepped into the water which she left running for him. Moira was in sparkling form, as if she had been revitalised by his absence. He could not bring himself to think that it might be due to her seeing another man. Wearing a calf-length skirt cut on the bias, a blouse and jacket, both loosely cut, she could have passed for a year or two older than Lucy.

The outfit, he realised, was new. It was another danger sign. Ian was not fashion-conscious himself: most of his clothes Moira chose. Perhaps now was the appropriate time to alter his attitude.

By ten thirty it was hot and noisy in the Taj Mahal as most of the tables were full. Groups of younger men and women trooped in looking for food before they went on to one of the night-clubs. The evening passed smoothly enough; Barry and Ian, forbidden to discuss work, were both fairly quiet and their wives assumed it was because of the murder.

The cold night air was welcome as they walked down the High Street past the numerous fast food outlets which seemed to have sprung out of nowhere, stepping over the litter such premises produced. The pubs had closed and the disco patrons had already been swallowed into their world of deafening sound and flashing lights. They said goood-night to the Swans, whose flat was more central, and turned the corner by a set of traffic signals. 'Isn't it mild?' Moira commented as if trying to make conversation with someone she hardly knew. 'We haven't had such a good winter for ages.'

'I wouldn't call it mild, love. Besides, February's usually worse.'

Moira slipped an arm through his, not a gesture she was entirely comfortable with as public displays of affection embarrassed her slightly, but Ian was troubled. Ian, whose hands were in his pockets, squeezed it with the inside of his elbow and felt flattered.

'Are you going in tomorrow?'

'Maybe. For an hour or so. Why?'

'I thought I'd start spring-cleaning if you were.'

Once more he felt rebuffed. She might as well have said she didn't want him around. He wondered if he could cope with the way his marriage was going.

It was WPC Judy Robbins' cheerful face which helped improve his mood on Sunday morning. There had been no necessity to go in, someone would have contacted him if there was any news. 'Here, grouchy,' she said, placing a mug of coffee on the desk. When she first came to Rickenham Green she had babysat for Mark. Ian was a sergeant then and had imagined that at least one other child would follow, but as the years slipped by and their lifestyle was adapted to their own tastes he and Moira decided it was too late to start again. Although she had been deeply attached to her father, Judy was part of the family. Fred Robbins had died the previous year and she was only just recovering from her loss. After serious consideration she had moved from her small flat to the bungalow he had inhabited and left to her in his will. The diversion of redecorating was helping her through moments of panic and loneliness.

'Grouchy? Less of that, young lady.' Ian managed a wan smile and noticed the smudges of tiredness under her eyes. 'Are you OK?'

'Yes, I'm fine. I didn't finish papering the spare room until after midnight then I decided I deserved a glass of wine and something to eat. I change shifts tomorrow so I can have a lie-in and catch up on sleep.'

Ian pictured the bungalow as Fred had left it: shabby, the paintwork in need of cleaning, if not painting, but relatively tidy. Judy would allow no visitors until she had redone every room. It made Ian think. 'Judy, you live on your own, who would you let into your house?'

'Friends, the gas man, people like that . . . hang on, this is to do with the murder, isn't it? But it's different for me – being in this job I'm aware of the dangers and I know what precautions to take. Other women might not be so careful. And I always ask for identification. Mind you, you can't always be sure it's genuine. Do you suppose that's what happened?'

'It's the only possibility as far as I'm concerned. We're checking now with the gas and electricity people.'

Judy shrugged. 'Good luck. I must go.'

Ian went down to the control room and asked to be

informed the minute any new information came in. At one o'clock he drove home and found Moira in jeans and a sweatshirt clearing out cupboards. They would, she said, be having their main meal in the evening.

3

The converted farmhouse was half-way down Broomhill Lane. It had been tastefully renovated without the addition of ugly extensions and, outwardly, was no different from when it was built over two hundred years ago.

Ian's hands were shaking as he got out of the car; the keys fell to the gravelled path. To the left of the building the old stable block stood open. It was now a garage, an expensive model parked perfectly straight between the upright beams. Wood smoke drifted across from a house set lower in the decline, its chimney barely visible through the trees. Beyond the house the sun was already dropping in the sky, the vivid gashes of orange and pink on the horizon bifurcated by the stark, bare branches of the trees which crested a distant hill.

The air was still yet there were no sounds other than the static crackles and hisses from a two-way radio. Outside lights were on but were more welcoming than illuminating as the gloom was not deep enough for the rays to be effective. Unnecessarily, in Ian's opinion, a warning lamp swirled on a patrol car, its cold blueness sweeping across tree trunks and his own face. The sickness in his stomach made itself known again and he tried not to think he was heading for some sort of breakdown. Another murder. A second woman dead. And Moira was going out again tonight.

He approached the house slowly, knowing what it held. When the call was put through to the control room Ian had not hesitated before calling out the team. It was not the way in which things were done – he, or someone, was supposed to

34

go to the scene first. But he had not wanted to waste a second, and he knew he would be proved right.

Virginia Baxter was in the kitchen, her long red hair spread like a sunburst over the varnished wood floor and spilling on to the edge of a multi-coloured cotton rug. She was not alone. The kitchen was large enough to allow those already present to work without getting in each other's way. Doc Harris's unmistakable rounded shape was visible through the kitchen window as he stood outside dragging on one of the numerous cigarettes he smoked each day.

John Cotton, bent to his task, glanced up and shrugged. No one had been keen to get things under way. When they arrived there were two PCs and a distraught husband but no sign of an inspector or the Chief.

Ian took one look at Virginia's face and nodded. He had not yet spoken. 'It's the same , isn't it?'

'Yes,' John Cotton replied resolutely, 'I'm afraid it is.'

Ian went out of the back door. 'Here, we're far enough away.' The Doc thrust a crumpled packet of Benson and Hedges in his direction. 'It's worrying.' There was no need for further consultation; both men were aware of what this might mean. It was too coincidental to believe two men, two husbands, had come home during the afternoon in order to strangle their wives then immediately telephoned the police. Ian lit the cigarette; there was no wind to flicker the flame, only a coldness which seemed to be seeping into his bones.

Calmer, Ian returned to the house. The lounge had once been two rooms but the original windows, or replicas, had been retained. There was an open fireplace as well as radiators and the classic furniture was in soft tones. Despite their obvious wealth – Ian knew roughly what properties in this area fetched – there was no ostentation; no silver-framed family photographs, no bows or flounces holding back the curtains, which fell straight to the floor. It was the sort of home Ian would have liked if he had ever thought about it.

Upstairs were four bedrooms. It was curiosity which led him there, he knew he would find nothing disturbed. There

35

were also two bathrooms, one of which was en suite in what he assumed was the Baxters' bedroom. The windows had security locks, as did all the outside doors, none of which had been disturbed. This woman, too, had willingly let her killer into the house and no doubt the post-mortem, as it had done in Debbie Orchard's case, would show there had been no struggle.

Ian's mind was barely functioning. He went back downstairs and into the lounge. On a table near the window were papers or documents, beside them, an open briefcase. He touched none of these things but saw the spread-out papers held designs of what had to be small ornaments or jewellery.

The Doc frowned when he saw Ian's expression but made no comment. Something was bothering his friend, something more than a double murder, but now was not the time to discuss it. Ian exchanged a few more words and left the team to their thankless task of discovering nothing. He was certain it would be so.

The husband, Clive Baxter, was sitting silently in the patrol car with an equally silent PC for company. The officer dared not leave Baxter alone in case he decided to take off, although he did not look as if he had the energy. Ian spoke briefly to him. Baxter nodded before returning his gaze to the house.

Ian drove back into Rickenham Green and dialled his home number. There was no reply. He spoke to Superintendent Thorne, requesting more manpower, and was told he would see what he could do. Then it was time to interview Baxter. He summoned up every bit of his own strength; his life was not good at the moment but whatever happened he had the chance to put things right. Baxter did not.

Barry Swan had had the afternoon off to take Lucy shopping in Ipswich. She worked some Saturdays in the bank and had a week-day off in lieu. It had been an enjoyable afternoon. After a latish lunch in a wine bar they strolled around the warm, brightly lit shops, buying little but happy just the same. Barry was still wearing his coat when he answered the telephone. 'Oh, shit!' he said, partly in exasperation at having

36

to go in but more in horror of what they might have on their hands. 'I'm sorry, Lucy, I can't say what time I'll be home.'

'It's all right.' She had known from the start what to expect because Judy Robbins had been her friend since schooldays and Judy had had to cancel the odd trip to the cinema or a meal out.

Clive Baxter, after telephoning the police, had not been able to bring himself to stay in the house. He waited outside, coatless, until they turned up. Now he sat in Ian's office, the interview rooms being too austere for an initial interview. His emotions seemed to be under control but Ian noticed the give-away signs. The man's face was ashen and had somehow sunk in upon itself, his hands shook and when he spoke he transposed the first letters of certain words, slurring as if he was drunk. He was almost as tall as Ian, his hair, neatly cut, almost all grey. He wore a business suit and his shoes were highly polished.

Ian placed his own chair on the same side of the desk. The man could not be entirely ruled out as a suspect but Ian had his own ideas.

'I went home for my papers and my overnight bag,' he was saying. 'Ginny, my wife, packed it for me because I was pushed for time and I had to catch a flight to Schipol. Amsterdam,' he added, so used to international airports he forgot others were not always as well versed.

Ian did not ask at that point why he had simply not taken it with him in the morning; he was letting him tell it in his own way.

'I left the car at the front of the house, opened the door and called out. I was surprised Ginny didn't come to greet me, she would have heard the car, you see. I called out again and then I went into the lounge, then the kitchen.' He stopped, his lips pressed firmly together to stop himself having to say what came next. As if performed by a perfectly timed stage direc-tion, there was a gentle tap at the door and an officer entered bearing a tray with two cups of coffee and a bowl of sugar. 'Thank you,' Ian said.

Baxter picked up the coffee, the cup rattling in the saucer before he took a sip. 'Would it be all right for me to smoke?'

'Of course.' Ian took an ashtray from his drawer and placed it on the desk. Baxter was not only elegant in appearance, his manners matched. Distraught as he was, he offered the packet to Ian. Twin plumes of smoke rose to meet the heat from the light over their heads before either man spoke again. It was dark outside, the traffic building up and becoming congested but unheard through the double-glazed windows.

'She was just lying there,' Baxter said. 'I thought that she'd fainted, or knocked herself out somehow. I wanted to think that, you see, I had to because . . .' He could not say, because the minute he saw her he knew she was dead. 'I shook her. Oh, God forgive me I slapped her face.' He put the cup and saucer on the desk and squeezed his eyelids with thumb and forefinger then shook his head, attempting to clear it of images which were fixed there for ever. 'I shouldn't have done that, I know that now. I shouldn't have touched her.'

No, Ian thought, you shouldn't. And I'm a policeman and if it was Moira lying on our kitchen floor I'd have done exactly the same thing. Baxter's grief touched him, made him more aware of what he might be losing. Right then he felt he might weep.

'There were no signs of forced entry, Mr Baxter, and I have seen your security system – your wife must have let someone in.'

'That's what I don't understand. She wasn't expecting anyone. It might sound arrogant of me to say we knew each other's movements, but it was an extra safeguard, in case of kidnap. That was always my worst fear because, at times, I have access to stones which can be converted into vast sums of money. She was only expecting me and I have my own key. Emma would have been there in the morning, but she leaves at twelve.'

'Emma?'

'She's a girl from Little Endesleigh, she comes in to help with the housework and do the occasional bits of shopping. There's not much difference in age between her and Ginny, they were more like friends really. I suppose you'll have to speak to her.'

Ian made a note of her address. 'And your wife worked from home, you say. Did she ever meet your colleagues or business associates?'

'Sometimes. She designs a lot of our jewellery, she has a natural flair for seeing how certain stones should be set. There's never been a real need for her to come to the office but she always likes to meet the people she deals with. Sometimes she accompanies me on trips abroad but usually I'm only away overnight and as deals are discussed over dinner, it isn't much fun for her.'

Ian asked him to make a list of all the people they both knew, professionally and otherwise, even though he believed it would be a waste of time. 'Not now,' he continued; 'when you feel up to it. What about neighbours, do you know them well?'

'Our lane is hardly used because it's the third side of a triangle with two B roads. The only people who use it are residents, it doesn't even cut the corner off because it winds so much. Sorry, I'm not really digressing, I was just thinking that if someone turned up in a car it's possible one of them might have noticed. We've two sets of neighbours to our left – the Connors, they're getting on a bit, Albert's virtually a cripple so they don't get out very much, and Tom and Jean Marsh. We don't have much to do with them, they're a bit, well, a bit common. They don't go out to work. There's a son but I can't remember his name.'

Ian would soon find out. 'And the other side?'

'A farm, a working farm, that is. Pete Morris is a good chap and his wife's nice. He bought most of our land before we moved in. He and his wife are in and out all day. They've got three youngsters, only one of them's at school. I don't know about the last house. It's been empty for a while but someone has bought it. I suspect it's going to be a holiday home.'

The next few questions related to strange telephone calls and unusual incidents but Baxter had had enough. Ian saw him downstairs to the revolving doors. 'Don't you want to know where you can find me?' There was no relief in the gaunt face at knowing he was apparently not under suspicion. 'I'll be at the Duke of Clarence, they're bound to have a room at this time of year.' He did not want to leave; standing there in the brightly lit reception, time and emotions could be frozen. 'What's wrong with me, Chief Inspector? I've lost the only person I care about and I can't damned well cry.'

'You will,' Ian said, laying a hand on his shoulder. 'You will.'

Baxter seemed not to hear as he went out into the night.

DS Swan had arrived too late to be part of the interview. Instead, he listened to Ian's version of it. 'He seems like a decent bloke from what you've said.'

'He is, I'm sure of it. And I'm damned certain he didn't kill her. But looking on the positive side, there is a pattern of sorts. None of this is coincidence – you know my views on that phenomenon. We have two victims, both female, both roughly the same age, and both bodies were discovered by their husbands. Now, we've no way of knowing if that was deliberate, if someone set out to ensure that was the case. Both women work, yet both were home during the afternoon. Mrs Baxter, by the way, designed jewellery for her husband's firm. You noticed how clean and tidy the Orchards' place was. It was the same at the Baxters', and both families are childless.'

'But their backgrounds are different?'

'It would seem so.'

'And you say Mrs Baxter has long red hair.' Barry did not need to elucidate. Certain men had fixations for a particular colour of hair. Debbie's hair was brown.

'The odd thing is, both of them allowed their killer in and there're no signs of a struggle. Both were strangled from behind, and that's unusual – a certain amount of anatomical knowledge is required if that's to be done successfully and quickly without a stocking or a garotte or somthing.' And this

40

was their first piece of information about the killer. 'Well, that's my lot for the day. I just can't take any more in.' Ian took his sheepskin coat from behind the door and shrugged it on. He ran a hand through his springy hair, hesitated, then picked up the outside telephone. There was still no reply at home.

And there was still no frost, although the temperature outside was a lot lower than the centrally heated office. To Ian's right was the brick wall of the side of the building, ahead, the road leading to the bypass; beyond where his car was parked a curving row of lights illuminated the dual carriageway. He pulled the sheepskin tighter, enjoying the leathery smell of it. Moira had bought it for him two Christmases ago after she had thrown his old, battered and torn one away. He had been furious at the time but now he intended to take more care with his clothes. He did not realise that although he did not have the *élan* of Barry Swan he always appeared clean and smart.

He unlocked the car. He wanted a drink. No, he needed a drink. But tonight he was not in the mood to join Campbell and Emmanuel and Markham in the Three Feathers, known to them all as the Feathers. It was at the top of the High Street; his favourite, the Crown, was on the Green, once the original hamlet of Rickenham Green. All that was left now was the pub and an oak tree, encircled with a wooden bench in the middle of the grass. The surrounding cottages had conserva-tion orders on them, as did the church, St Luke's, incongruous now amongst the supermarkets and building societies, but still a reminder of a more gentle age. St Luke's was small and picturesque with its spire and lych-gate, and a popular venue for weddings. The churchyard had long since been obsolete and backing on to it was Safeway's car-park. Behind it, on the rolling hills where sheep and cattle once grazed, were the staggered roofs of a council estate. Ian's mental eyes continued travelling around the town. There were back-street pubs but they would be noisy with their juke-boxes and pool tables, and the Elms Country Club was too far out. The Doc fre-quented it; he was a member and played golf there and was

41

well known and respected, despite his penchant for large Scotches. The George, he thought. He hadn't been in there for years. He had heard there were new people in charge. It used to be a fine place for business lunches – good food served in a quiet atmosphere, the music classical, the wine drinkable – but that trade had been gradually dying out.

He drove the short distance across town to Saxborough Road, trying not to think about the cases, and indicated left. There were no parking restrictions here so he pulled into the kerb and killed the ignition. Hoping it had not been turned into a theme pub or one which catered for youngsters, Ian approached the George. It did not look any different. He crossed the foyer; the furnishings were still maroon plush, the carpet, although new, much in the style of the old one and the pleasant, curving bar had not been altered. He needed the Gents, but like most people, not wishing to appear rude, bought his drink before using the facilities. The armchairs were of the studded leather variety and the area behind the bar gleamed, bottles and glasses reflected in the mirrored shelves. He looked up to receive his change and thank the barman. He gripped the counter, his head spinning. In those mirrors he had just been admiring he saw Moira return from the back of the room and take a seat. With her was a man, one he did not know. She leant forward, listening eagerly to what he was saying, then laid a hand over his. For a second he wanted to run, to get out of the place and make himself believe it had not happened, but his slight movement had caught her eye. She had seen him.

He picked up his glass and walked to their table.

'Ian,' she said, her hand going to her throat in what he recognised to be a defensive gesture. 'Good heavens.' She laughed nervously. 'I didn't think you used this place.'

No amount of interrogation, no amount of bullying could have elicited such a perfect admission of guilt.

'I don't. Not usually. I fancied a quiet drink. I see you did, too.'

'Ian, this is John Freeling, my boss. John, this is my husband.

Ian, sit down and join us. You don't mind, do you?' John Freeling shook his head, apparently not in the least concerned about the situation. The tense atmosphere was almost palpable. Moira tried to make conversation but failed. Neither man was interested in small talk.

Ian drank his pint rapidly, blinding rage and humiliation vying for superiority. It was bad enough that he did not have the nerve to demand to know what was going on – worse, he would not make a scene in public, embroil himself in some ugly fracas, in case he got his name in the papers and a disciplinary hearing at work. He tried to convince himself that he was being sensible but the words 'moral coward' came to mind immediately.

It was Moira who did the sensible thing. 'Look, John, I'm sorry about this but I'll have to go now. I hope everything works out. I'll see you tomorrow.' She stood. It was up to Ian, he could follow her or not. John had brought her in the car; if Ian stayed, or went elsewhere, she would walk home or get the bus. Her own temper was only just under control. She heard Ian's gruff 'Goodbye' as he came after her.

The car was down the road a little way. Moira walked towards it. 'Isn't your boyfriend taking you home?' Ian said as he caught her up.

She ignored him and stood patiently by the passenger door, seeing from his expression that he wanted to drive off without her. 'Get in,' he said. They did not exchange another word until they were inside the house.

Moira unlocked the door and put on the lights before heading straight to where they kept the drinks in the living-room. She poured a glass of wine but did not offer Ian a drink. She could tell that the pint in the George had been his first, that he was as sober as herself.

Ian stood in the doorway, still in his coat. 'I am working on two murders,' he said coldly. 'Yes, there has been a second. Two women, both killed in their own homes. And do you know what? For the first time in my career as a policeman I can fully understand why it happens.'

43

Moira sipped her drink, her own gaze equally cold, but said nothing.

'I see. You can't even be bothered to lie to me, to make up some excuse. It might've been kinder if you had.'

Outwardly Moira remained calm. Had this been anyone else, a suspect, a victim, a witness, Baxter or Orchard, anyone else at all, he would immediately have known that he was witnessing an enormous effort at self-control. But this was Moira, and Moira was his wife, and that had always been the problem. 'How long's it been going on?' he asked. 'Answer me, woman, will you? It is you I'm talking to. How long have you been having it off with your boss?'

It took less than a second for Moira to cover the few yards between them and in the same movement she jerked her wrist, throwing the contents of her glass into Ian's face. A small sound escaped from her throat but she did not speak.

Ian, wiping his face and lapels with a handkerchief, was stunned. He heard her footsteps loudly on the stairs and the slamming of Mark's bedroom door. 'Fine,' he said aloud. 'Fine. If that's the way she wants it.' He poured a generous measure of whisky, Debbie Orchard and Virginia Baxter temporarily forgotten. One thing was certain, he was going to have it out with her, but in his own time. Let her stew, she was the one in the wrong. Accepted he did not make as much effort as he could and perhaps he was no longer such a good catch, but there was still no excuse for it. And to be so blatant! Someone from work might have seen her. No, she had admitted she had chosen the George because none of them used it. He poured a second drink. It was all bravado. He wasn't going to have it out with her, he did not want to lose her. The affair would surely run its course. He had known men who put up with far worse than this.

His anger evaporated and the second, even larger drink only made him full of self-pity. He wished for a return of the old days, when Moira was content to be at home, when the meals were always on time and she did not go out in the evenings except with Deirdre or to one of the charity things

44

she did. But what had she done with herself all day then? Had there been others? Some blame must be attached to him, he knew that. When did he ever ask what she had been doing, or listen to the answer if he did? 'You're not interested in what I do,' she had once said to him sadly. 'I know how involved you are with work, but I do have a life too, you know.'

No, he thought, I won't, as an unfamiliar tightness gripped his throat and tears burned behind his eyes. He poured another drink because he had not cried since he was a child and he was not about to start now.

A sliver of daylight showed between the gap in the curtains. It was after eight. The level of whisky in the bottle told him what sort of day to expect before he became aware of his hangover. He had slept in the chair, warm from the waist up because he was still wearing his coat, but his feet were cold. The dryness of his mouth and stickiness of his eyes were apparent before the thumping began in his head and, despite his emergency treatment, there were stains on the sheepskin. How was he going to face Moira?

He went to the kitchen and filled the kettle, drinking three glasses of grapefruit juice before it boiled. Nervously, he made tea and carried a mug upstairs, forgetting for a moment that Moira had gone into Mark's room. He shut their bedroom door; the duvet, neatly spread, the top sheet tucked back over it, was like an accusation. Rarely did they sleep apart, only when Moira stayed with her mother or if one of them had a cough or a cold when Ian would sleep on the settee.

Mark's door was ajar. He nudged it open. That bed, too, was made. Moira was not in the bathroom either. He could smell the lemony tang of the frequent-wash shampoo she used and the mirror was still steamed over. She had gone to work, gone out into the darkness without saying goodbye. His stomach contracted. It was more serious than he had imagined. When they argued they made it up the same day, or at

45

least the following morning. But had she gone to work? What if she was not coming back at all?

'You're late,' Barry said, surprised. 'Couldn't you get to sleep last night?' He had had problems himself, thinking about the double murders.

'No, I slept all right.' Too long, that was the trouble, and too deeply, or he might have had a chance to speak to Moira.

Each hour seemed more like two. Every so often Ian's hand rested on the telephone receiver; each time he removed it without dialling Moira's work number. His will-power had never been so stretched as he made himself concentrate on the two women who were no longer in a position to be unfaithful to their husbands.

The second murder, although not planned like the first, had been too good an opportunity to miss. He laughed. He had believed he knew Rickenham Green and the surrounding villages like the back of his hand. He had been wrong. He did not like being wrong, or made to feel as if he was. But what an opportunity his mistake had provided, what a brilliant piece of luck.

And her smile when she had let him in. What a fool she was, and how trusting. All that security and none of it had saved her. Didn't they read the papers? Hadn't they heard that DCI, speaking from the steps of the police station, warning women to be careful? But the DCI had looked more shifty than any criminal, perhaps they hadn't taken him seriously. The second statement had been made from higher up: Superintendent Thorne had far more presence about him and seemed more comfortable in front of the media.

She had died very quickly. It surprised him, just as it had the first time. It was fine knowing something in theory, practice was usually a different matter.

He would wait a while now, let the heat die down. And, meanwhile, he had other distractions.

4

DS Markham, built like a highly trained Marine, hair uncompromisingly short, was a loner. He lived alone and he worked alone whenever he could. That was the way he preferred it. It was also, mostly, the way his colleagues preferred it. Not that he was disliked – it was just that his taciturn manner and long silences were hard to live with. Many men had tried, and failed, to fill them with inconsequential chatter. Yet there were times, especially in the pub, when he would utter one short sentence of such ironic perception or acerbic wit that it would make them laugh.

He had had women, but never for long. His idea of romance was not theirs and his fearless attitude, his control, his never letting go, scared them. It had scared men too.

It was DS Markham who was sent the day after Virginia Baxter's death to see Emma Dearing.

Emma lived with her grandmother in one of the new bungalows in Little Endesleigh. Everyone still referred to them as that although they had been built more than five years ago.

'She's lived with me since she was eight,' Maggie Evans, the grandmother, informed him. 'Her father did a bunk when she was a baby, and my daughter, well, least said about her the better. I haven't heard from her in years and she's never even sent Emma a birthday card. Poor little dear, she was in a right state when she first came here. Afraid of everything she was. Thank God for the village school, that's what I say, three years there before she went on to Rickenham did wonders for her. We're campaigning to save it, you know.'

47

'Yes, I did know.'

Mrs Evans chattered on as she led him to the kitchen, which was modern but homely. They had lived in Vicarage Road until they moved here three years ago. Markham could smell cooking – casserole or cottage pie. It would be home-made. 'She'll be home soon, she only has a couple of tutorials a week. Now, I expect you'd like a nice cup of something?'

'Coffee, please, black, no sugar.'

They were seated for no more than five minutes before Emma came through the back door, surprised to see a visitor.

Markham introduced himself, realising that Emma would not have let him in as readily as her grandmother had done, and certainly not without showing some form of identification. She was as upset as he had been warned she would be on hearing that Virginia Baxter was dead.

'She was a good friend to me,' Emma told him when she was more composed. 'I only saw her yesterday, she was fine, she was laughing.'

'Emma, did anything unusual happen yesterday, telephone calls or visitors?'

She shook her head. 'Clive was in one of his panics in the morning. Ginny always laughed about it, he was forever putting things in a safe place and then not being able to find them. He was going to Amsterdam and he'd mislaid the papers he needed. Ginny said we'd find them. He had an early call to make in Ipswich so she said for him to go on and she'd pack his bag and he could collect everything later. Oh!' Emma's eyes widened. 'Clive won't know.'

She must have assumed that the murder had taken place after Clive returned, but she had answered the question the Chief had forgotten to ask – why did Baxter need to return home that afternoon? 'It was Mr Baxter who found his wife.'

'Poor Clive.' She hesitated. 'I really can't understand it, Ginny wasn't expecting anyone. I used to check her diaries for her. Besides, I'd help with food and drinks or whatever, and she wouldn't let anyone in she didn't know. Clive was always going on about that.'

48

'Do you have a key?'

'No. It's not that they don't trust me, it's to do with the insurance or something.'

Markham had been expecting this answer. They had already checked that neither woman had lost keys, or a handbag containing keys which might also contain their address. He studied Emma, pale now with red-rimmed eyes. She was sturdy yet delicate, her light brown hair tied back in a band. 'How many days do you go to the Baxters'?'

'Three. I'm doing a part-time course at Rickenham Tech, you see, and it fits in perfectly. Gran didn't want me to work as well, but I can't let her keep me, not at my age, and I gave up a full-time job to study.'

'I told her she'll make herself ill, trying to do too much, but she won't listen.'

'It's not too much, and you know it. What I did for Ginny could hardly be described as hard work. What'll I do?' she asked, addressing Markham. 'I'm supposed to go there tomorrow. Will Clive want me there, do you think?'

'I really don't know. It might be best to wait and see if he contacts you.'

She nodded and Markham said he would be in touch if they needed any further information. Emma Dearing came across as an ordinary, straightforward sort of person, one who was unaccustomed to lying.

Markham made his way back to headquarters.

'It's hard to comprehend,' Ian said when Markham reported back. 'Surely whoever killed these women can't have been aware of how little time he had. Debbie returns at three fifty, according to her neighbour, and her husband returns an hour later. Emma Dearing is with Ginny until twelve thirty then Baxter returns just after three. Two cases in which we didn't need the pathologist to narrow down the margins of time of death.' Ian felt a great need to talk it over with Moira, to speculate, to allow her the chance to put her views which, seen from an outside perspective, were sometimes clearer than his own. But he could not do so tonight; there were other pressing domestic matters to deal with first.

'Is DC Campbell about?'

'He's in the control room.'

'Send him up, would you?'

Alan Campbell was the archetypal Scotsman: blue eyes, sandy hair, with a matching thin moustache and ginger freckles. His Glaswegian accent, which he claimed was hardly noticeable, sounded broad to other ears. He had taken a few knocks in life but instead of becoming more dour, which was his natural demeanour, he had mellowed. He still remained pedantic, though.

'We've got all their personal stuff now, haven't we?' Ian asked when he appeared.

'Yes, sir. Diaries, desk diaries, bank statements, the lot.'

'Good. I want you to do your thing with the computer. Feed every bit of the information in and see if there's anything, anything at all, which is common to both women. How long do you think it'll take?'

'No more than a couple of hours.'

Campbell went to do so. These items had already been checked manually but something might have been missed – a telephone number, perhaps, listed by both women but beside a different name. It was unlikely, but not impossible. Meanwhile Ian wanted to read what Baxter's neighbours had to say. The words blurred each time he thought of Moira. Still he had not rung her.

It was eight o'clock before he could reasonably leave that evening. Ian bypassed the pub, unable to do anything more until he knew where he stood.

Through the window of the house opposite his own he saw two children playing. The curtains had not yet been drawn and a television set flickered in the corner. They were young to be up so late but as he locked the car a woman came into view, switched off the set and took them both by the hand. Presumably it was bedtime. Ian did not know the people because they had only recently moved in. The scene was so normal, so everyday, and must be happening in thousands of homes throughout the country. Not so behind his own front door, which he dreaded opening. But light showed through the coloured fanlight. He took a deep breath. Moira was home.

Conscientiously, not wanting to get anything wrong, he hung up his coat, placed his briefcase under the hall table and his keys on top of it just as Moira always advised, to save time searching for them in the mornings. The fire, but not the light, was on in the living-room. He heard sounds from the kitchen and opened the door. Moira was at the sink, her back to him. She had heard him come in and now saw his reflection in the window but did not turn round.

'Moira? I think we need to talk.'

'There's nothing to say.' Her voice was flat.

'How can you say that?' Ian felt his anger beginning to rise but controlled it.

'Quite easily. What time would you like to eat?'

He sat at the table, defeated. He had never known her to be like this, so cold and uncaring and seemingly unaware of his pain.

'Last night. I didn't mean it to come out like that. It was a shock, as I'm sure you can imagine, finding you with him like that.' He refused to use John Freeling's name.

'All right,' Moira said, finally turning around. She leaned against the edge of the sink, her arms folded. 'All right. It was a shock. I expect it was. Because you see, my life doesn't count, does it?'

'I . . . but you – '

'You want to talk, then let me.' Her voice had risen. 'I've told you each time when I'm going out. Not once have you thought to inquire where. One evening I went over to Lucy's, another time to Deirdre's. It isn't very exciting sitting alone most evenings.'

'Moira, there was another murder – '

51

'Yes. Precisely. And you, and you alone, are responsible for finding the murderer, I suppose. I know that's how you see it. And when you're in that frame of mind – no, as we're being honest here, mostly – you don't hear a word I say. I have deliberately not told you what I've been doing lately. And then, what you said last night, I simply couldn't believe it.' She was fast losing control of her temper. 'How dare you! How dare you accuse me like that! If one of your precious criminals was caught red-handed you still wouldn't jump to conclusions. You'd ask questions, make inquiries, get proof, and even then you'd tread carefully before you charged him. Not so with me though, is it? I know you're respected as a fair man at work but that side of you is not apparent at home. I shall tell you what I was doing last night even though you don't deserve an explanation. John Freeling has been in a bad way since the weekend. I asked him what the matter was and he asked if I'd have a drink with him because he didn't want to discuss it in the office. He needed someone to talk to, he said, someone who was happily married.' She laughed scornfully. 'Little does he know. John's wife walked out and took the children with her. She said it was because he wasn't paying them enough attention, he didn't listen because he was so wrapped up in the business. He had just told me all that when you walked in so I wasn't much use to him after all.'

Ian stood up and took a step towards her.

'One more thing,' she added. 'If you don't get your act together, it won't be only John's wife who walks out.'

'You don't mean that.'

'I do.'

'Oh, God, I'm so sorry.' Everything she had said was true, especially the part about giving other people the benefit of the doubt. 'Really I am. All the time we were in France, and after, I'd convinced myself there was someone else. Forgive me, Moira. Please?'

She softened slightly but was not about to tell him that she had been pleased to come home after the holiday because, like

52

him, she enjoyed working and intended doing more with her life – it was not the case, as he believed, that her whole world revolved around him and his moods.

'Look, leave the food. We'll go out, just the two of us. Somewhere special. I'll make it up to you, I promise.'

'I don't want to go out, Ian. I want to spend an ordinary evening at home with a man who will listen to what I am saying, one who does not simply grunt or nod in what he thinks is the appropriate place. Now excuse me, I want to lay the table.'

Ian moved out of the way and went to open some wine, an expensive bottle he had been saving. His emotions were once more in conflict. Relief was uppermost but Moira was changing, had changed, since she had started work, and he was not sure where it would end. He knew it was now up to him.

In the morning DC Campbell told Ian he could find nothing to connect the two women. He had stayed later than was necessary to double check. 'We're going further back,' he said, 'to when they were younger.' It might be they had a shared acquaintance, one who held a grudge

DS Swan replaced Campbell as soon as he left. 'The last of the lab reports on the Orchard case. They're meaningless as they stand but when the Baxter reports come through we might find a connection between them.' But they both believed whoever it was knew what he was doing; no hairs at the scene, no fingerprints, no nothing.

Virginia Baxter's parents were flying home that day. They had been in Spain to spend the winter in their villa. The police now knew she had a brother, a fact which Clive Baxter had omitted to mention. They also knew the brother had spent several months in prison. 'A bit of a Raffles type' is how he was described. 'Country houses, knew what he was looking for.' But that was ten years ago.

Ian wondered if he had been blackmailing his sister or maybe she had refused to bail him out and he had killed her.

53

Possible, but that did not explain Debbie Orchard's death. They were still trying to find the brother but all they had was an eight-year-old address for lodgings in Cambridge.

'I want every tradesman, every visitor to both those properties in the last year interviewed,' Ian said. 'Milkmen, postmen, delivery men, every damned one of them.'

'What about take-away deliveries?' Barry suggested. 'No, I don't suppose the Baxters dined on Chicken Madras in tinfoil.'

'Why not?' Ian was indignant. 'Nothing wrong with that.'

They were now working on the possibility that a regular visitor, a postman for instance, who saw them daily and had a rough idea of their movements might be responsible. Someone who might recently have changed rounds, who would be recognised by a uniform – there was, after all, a second post now. The only discrepancy was that Debbie was killed in her living-room, Virginia in the kitchen, but if they had been asked to sign for something it might be where they kept a pen handy.

And then Roy Orchard telephoned. He had remembered that a month or so ago a man had come to the house to make some minor adjustment to the car. 'He came in for a cup of tea,' Orchard said. 'Debbie insisted because he looked cold. He couldn't fix it after all. He had to take the car away with him.'

Good, Ian thought. At last. But the optimisim was short-lived. Ian would have bet a substantial sum of money that the Baxters would take their cars to a large, reputable dealer to be serviced or repaired, not to a one-man band in a shabby outfit down near the disused railway sidings. However, it was better than nothing.

DS Emmanuel was sent to the relevant address. Almost as tall as the Chief, but very black, he was an intimidating figure unless you knew him or saw his smile. Having been in Rickenham Green for some years he was used to being stared at, unlike in the city where he had worked before but from which he had obtained a transfer. The city was getting him down and he had woman trouble. Amarella was married; her husband was a layabout and a slob and did not care if his wife was around or not. Amarella was supposed to have joined him but Winston Emmanuel had long since given up hope of that. They still spoke over the telephone but it was becoming harder to find things to say.

Not long after Judy Robbins' father died he had taken her out for a meal to cheer her up, surprised that she had accepted the invitation. They got on well, he liked and admired her despite her feisty ways, but they both knew friendship was the limit of any possible relationship. Yes, he thought, as he pulled into the scruffy yard, it's time I found another woman.

He stepped straight into a puddle and cursed softly. It was not a good start. There was a battered van to one side of the yard and several other, newer cars awaiting repair. Scattered around were rusty door panels and wings. It was a dump. In the shed which acted as an office was a man in his fifties. He wore oil-streaked brown overalls and a greasy cap which was tilted back as he scratched his scalp. Overhead was an unshaded light bulb which only emphasised the dilapidation of the place. The desk was littered with paperwork, curling at the edges and smudged with dirty fingermarks. The only thing which was alien was the calendar on the wall showing a picture of a local stately home instead of the obligatory nude.

'Yes?' The man spoke with an almost total lack of interest, as if smartly dressed, tall, black men walked in every day of the week.

'Are you Mr Proctor, the proprietor of this business?'

'Happen I am, son. Who is it wants to know?' The accent was broad Yorkshire and sounded strange to Winston's ears now he was used to the soft Suffolk burr. He showed his identity which, in turn, produced no reaction. Proctor had nothing to hide; there was no guilty start, no shifty expression and no protests of innocence, only the same bland indifference. 'You'd best take a seat then,' he said. Proctor removed some tools from the only other seat and placed them on the floor.

'What's it about? I don't buy and sell cars, only fix 'em. I wouldn't know if one was knocked off or not.'

'It's a bit more serious than that, sir. You must be aware that we're investigating the death of – '

'Bloody 'ell. I saw it on the telly. You don't think I did them in?'

DC Emmanuel refrained from answering. He was their only lead. 'I believe you were called out to repair Mr Orchard's car. Alexander Road. About two months ago.'

'Was I?' Proctor scratched his scalp again then shoved his cap into place. 'You're telling me it was one of my customers 'as got herself killed? God, business is bad enough as it is. Orchard, you say? Now you mention it, it does ring a bell.' He pulled a ledger towards him and opened it, running a finger down the page, then repeated the exercise twice more, working backwards through the book. Business was not that bad, Winston noticed. 'Ah, here we are. You're right. But it were my son who collected the car, he does most of the graft now while I run this place.' He indicated the shabby room with a gesture as expansive as if it was a suite in a state-of-the-art office block.

'Where's your son now, Mr Proctor?'

'Out on a job. I don't suppose he'll be long, from what I gather it's only a minor repair.' He had another scratch. 'That's what most of our work consists of now, we're just scraping along, but I'm too young to retire and I don't want to lay my lad off. What else is he going to get these days?'

'How long do you call not long?'

Proctor looked at his watch. 'Another twenty minutes at most. You can stop on if you want, you won't be disturbing me, there's little enough to do here at the minute.'

'Thanks. Would you object if I had a look at your book?'

'Help yourself. There's nothing to hide.'

Winston swung it around and studied it whilst Proctor made tea. The mug was cracked but the tea was strong, even if the milk was tinned. He had not wanted to antagonise the man by asking but he needed to check whether the Baxters had also made use of his services. He began at the first page of the ledger, which was dated half-way through the previous year. The name Baxter did not appear but what did catch his eye was an address in Broomhill Lane. Here, it seemed, was the first thing which might connect the two women.

Jason Proctor returned fifteen minutes later.

Marian Thomas was in the process of reassessing her life and she was fighting against conflicting ideas. Jim had left her and, from a distance, she saw that the problem with their marriage had been more her fault than his. It was ironic in these times of equality that his complaint had been that she was indecisive, that she tried *too* hard and that her running around after him was irritating. Jim wanted an equal. He had moved into a small flat but there had been no mention of a divorce. They needed time, he said, but meanwhile they agreed to pursue their own lives. That had been almost a year ago.

Being on her own had taught Marian many things, not least of which was that she was capable and growing into a responsible adult able to control her own life. Her efforts had earned her a slightly higher position in the company for which she worked, an achievement she was proud of. Jim had been genuinely pleased when she telephoned to impart the news. There were no hard feelings and Jim had been surprised that Marian had not rung up every five minutes asking him to come over and mend something.

It was Jim Marian wanted but, although he was not seeing anyone, the reverse did not seem to apply. Then she had backed into a man in the supermarket and a loaf of bread fell from her basket. They had smiled at each other and made conversation as they waited at the check-out counter and she had accepted his invitation to go out for a drink.

She had met him twice more but she suspected that he counted women as inferior beings, and she was having second thoughts. It would be easy enough to get out of because the relationship had not progressed to a physical stage. It had puzzled her, men were no longer content to wait. They had made another arrangement to which she had agreed, proving that her metamorphosis was not quite complete because she had wanted to say no. Now the decision had been made. When he came she would explain she no longer wanted to see him because she was not ready for another relationship.

The day brought far more than Ian had hoped for. A report was faxed from Cambridge: Alastair Harvey, Virginia Baxter's brother, had lodged with a woman there for a year from the time he was released from prison. The plump and cheerful landlady remembered him as a gentleman, prompt with his rent and ready with his wit. She had no forwarding address, only a vague recollection of him mentioning he was going to his sister's, but who she was or where she lived was not known. It was enough. The search for Alastair Harvey was intensified.

Someone was sent to the hotel where Clive Baxter was still staying. He confirmed the existence of Harvey but said that he had had little to do with him and that he had never been to the house. 'It was his choice, not ours,' Baxter said. 'Ginny was very fond of him but he kept his distance. I think he felt he was an embarrassment to us. Or perhaps', he continued, as if the thought had only just occurred to him, 'it would have proved to be too much of a temptation.' Clive did not know his address, nor was it listed in any of his wife's personal effects. But neither was the British address of her parents, only the one belonging to their Spanish villa, which did not rule out the possibility that they were still in touch.

'But we've only the landlady's word for it. Harvey may have used it as an excuse, perhaps he never came here at all.'

'The senior Harveys might be able to tell us,' Barry said.

'True. Meanwhile, I've got work to do.' Other pressing matters were waiting on Ian's desk but he reckoned he could get through them within the hour. Barry went off to assist with tracing Harvey.

'Are you busy?' WPC Robbins poked her head around the door. It was a superfluous question. The paperwork remained half completed whilst Ian, hands clasped behind his head, leant back in the chair, its front legs tilted off the floor. 'I'm not stopping. I just wanted to know if you're likely to be late tonight.'

'Oh?' He smiled. 'Why's that? Are you propositioning me?'

'You're not my type. It's just that I haven't seen Moira for ages and now the decorating's done, I was going to ask her over and then go for a Chinese to celebrate.'

'Ah, I see. And you wanted to make sure we hadn't already got our own candlelit dinner planned.'

'Something like that.'

A small frown of uncertainty crossed his brow. 'Carry on. Either way she'll accept,' he said. And there was no reason why Moira should not accept. They had no plans and there had been many occasions when he had let her down at the last minute. But the doubts had reasserted themselves. Had Moira put Judy up to it, asked her to provide an alibi for whatever else she was doing? He was ashamed of the thought Moira would neither conceive of such an idea nor involve a friend in such deception and Judy would certainly not comply if she did.

The urgent reply to a memo regarding reorganisation must wait. He could not sit in the office any longer. He wanted some action.

A fine drizzle hung in the air, the annoying kind, too light to require the windscreen wipers on but damping enough to have to flick them every so often. There was the usual hold-up in the High Street as the driver of an articulated lorry misjudged the narrow gap between Boots and Marks and Spencer. There was an unloading area behind the shops but the manoeuvre was awkward, especially when cars were parked on the double yellow lines on both sides of the alley. And no bugger ever seems to do anything about it, Ian thought, exasperated. However, the driver, looking relieved, aligned cab and trailer and the warning bleep of his vehicle remained steady as he inched backwards. Ian took a short cut, turning left and coming out at the bottom of Deben Lane. He drove past the Bradley Court housing estate and cut back to the bypass. From there it was easy going as he joined the A12 to Ipswich. He was on his way to Baxter's offices simply because he wanted to get a feel of the place, of the people with whom he and his wife were involved.

He parked and went on foot the several hundred yards necessary. The drizzle had stopped. Rickenham had been congested, it was worse here. Buses lined up and were tooted at by irate drivers who could not get past, although it was their fellow motorists who were to blame. The bus-stops had acquired a new identity and were doubling as car-parking space. Ian grinned when he saw a traffic warden cross at the lights. Someone was going to be sorry.

The glass doors of the building were embellished with gleaming brass handles and opened on to an expanse of marble floor in the centre of which, swamped by its surroundings, was a desk. Behind it was a man in uniform, presumably protecting the bank of lifts at his rear. Ian scrutinised the board on the wall into which were pegged the names of the companies in the building and the floors on which they could be found.

'May I help you, sir?'

Ian turned around. 'Ah, yes. Maybe you can. He explained his business.

'A terrible thing to happen. Poor Mr Baxter , I don't know how he'll cope, he was devoted to his wife. Like I said to the chappie who interviewed me, we were all terribly shocked and upset. No one's been able to talk about anything else.'

Ian let him continue while he made a calculation. There were three floors above with, what? – four rooms on each, maybe five. At least fifty people must work here, probably more, yet the man at the desk made it sound as if everyone was on intimate terms. He smiled and adopted a relaxed pose, ready for a quiet little chat. Men like these were often worth cultivating.

'I expect you get to know them all pretty well?'

'Most of them. The secretaries, the younger ones, they don't take a lot of notice of me.' He smiled. 'More's the pity. And a couple of the younger men think the world would collapse without them, they do, with their raincoats and briefcases, rushing about like there's a fire.' He leant forward, warming to his theme. 'But then you get the people like Mr Baxter, they make up for it. Ask anyone and they'll tell you the same, always remembers to ask after the grandchildren. That's what I call real class. Mrs Baxter likewise.' He shook his head. 'I still can't believe it. Terrible world we live in nowadays, crime everywhere. If you ask me, what these youths need is a spell in the army. It didn't do me any harm, and . . . '

Ian saw it was time to stop him. He did so politely and made for the lift which, to his relief, took him smoothly and quickly up to the third floor.

Clive Baxter's offices were smart and tasteful but not as opulent as Ian had anticipated. They were decorated in much the same style as his home and he wondered if Ginny had had a hand in their design. A girl in her mid-twenties greeted him and said they did not know when Clive would be back. There were no particular questions he needed to ask so Ian sat back and let the girl talk, sensing more from her tone than from what she was saying. The staff got on well together with no personality clashes, Clive was respected and Ginny much admired, and once more he was told how happy the Baxters were.

Back in the street he realised he had been wasting time but the visit had taken him a step closer to the victim. He also knew he ought to have made a courtesy call to the Ipswich police to inform them of his intentions.

The Rickenham Green control room was relatively quiet and there was a lack of detectives around. DS Swan and DC Emmanuel were both in the interview rooms, each accompanied, which meant it was formal. Things had certainly been moving in his absence. He could not interrupt; he would have to wait until they had finished. As he was still on the ground level he might as well continue down to the canteen and get something to eat whilst he had a chance. It was way past lunchtime.

'Don't you ever have a day off, Betty?' he asked the woman behind the counter.

'I'm filling in for Sarah, she's got the flu. My husband's down with it too. Mind you, you'd think he'd got bubonic plague to hear him carry on. The chops aren't bad today,' she added.

'Go on then.' He handed over his money and carried his tray to a table. 'Judy, twice in one day. I'm flattered.'

'I've only come to get Sergeant Whitelaw a cup of tea. I heard Winston's interviewing a suspect.'

'A suspect?' Why hadn't he been told it was a suspect? Because I wasn't here, he reminded himself, and because, as Moira rightly pointed out, there are plenty of other people capable of handling things. 'Who told you?'

'Dunno. You know what it's like around here. If our grapevine bore fruit we'd be able to supply the world with wine.'

'Did you ring Moira?'

'Yes. We're going to the Lotus Blossom.'

'That's a bit upmarket, isn't it?'

'You've got to try these places. Anyway, I'm using the voucher from the *Herald*.' Judy went to get the tea and Ian began his meal. He had passed the new Chinese on his way to the coast. It was a large, one-storey building, recently opened and constructed on the site of what had once been a garage and transport café. It had been derelict for years, the ancient petrol pumps rusted, the windows boarded up and rust obliterating the name which had been painted on the green, corrugated metal roof. Resilient weeds had sprung up on the forecourt and broken through the surface. The new pagoda-style roof and the plastic tropical plants in the windows offended Ian's sensibilities, as did their price list, but he could see Judy's point. For the first month they were offering two meals for the price of one on presentation of the coupon from the paper.

Ian's patience was not rewarded when DC Emmanuel emerged from interview room 4. 'That was the lad who repaired the Orchards' car. Jason Proctor. I thought I'd discovered a connection, sir, he'd also done a job in Broomhill Lane some while ago for Pete Morris. He's got the farm next to Baxter's house. Roy Orchard got his name from a friend – recommendation's how the Proctors work these days, can't afford the advertising it seems, and Jason went to school with Morris. DS Markham confirmed it for me earlier. Morris always puts business his way when he can, and uses him himself. He said he knows what it costs to bring up young children.'

'And?'

'And I can't shake him, sir. He denies ever having been to the Baxters or knowing anything about them.'

'Is he lying?'

'I don't think so. We had to let him go.'

'Of course. Just the same, we'll keep our options open. He's the only person we've found who's had any kind of access to both addresses. Has Swan finished yet?'

'I don't know.'

'OK, thanks.'

'One more thing, sir. I brought the ledger in with me, neither of the Proctors objected. Campbell went through it. Jason Proctor was out at Little Endesleigh putting a new clutch in a Mrs Davenport's car for the whole of the afternoon of Virginia Baxter's death. She's confirmed the date and the times.'

Disappointment was tempered with hope. If they had found one connection they could find another.

'Tell me,' Ian said when Barry appeared, looking tired and running a hand through his hair.

'Easier to listen to the tape.'

Alastair Harvey had walked into the reception area just as more men were being instructed to help find him. DS Swan had taken him into an interview room, explained what he was doing and why, asked him if he understood or objected, and set the recording equipment going. He said who was in the room and gave the date and time. Harvey's voice was low and well modulated, his manner easy. Ian realised how easy it would have been for him to talk his way into invitations to country residences. Ex-villain or not, the man had charm and style. Ridiculous as it might be, Ian, without having met him, felt he would have liked him. Barry said he was technically better looking than his sister, his hair lighter, but reddish glints were visible under the strip lighting.

Harvey admitted he thought the police might be looking for him. 'I didn't realise it was as a suspect,' he said, 'only to inform me of the news. You see, I've only just read about it in the paper. My parents have no idea where I live but Ginny and I were very close when we were young, they would have wanted me to know.' Unbelievably, Harvey did not take a daily newspaper, nor did he watch television. The copy of the *Rickenham Herald* was several days old before he saw it, and he only read it then because it had been left in the shop by a visitor to Ipswich. This was the beginning of the interview. DS Swan decided to give him the benefit of the doubt; he did not want to antagonise him initially.

'You'll know about my previous history, but I've been straight ever since I came out. That's one experience I don't wish a second time. Still, I expect they all say that. But I've never been involved with violence.' A flicker of pain had crossed his face but Ian was unable to see all the physical nuances of the interview. Sometimes it was better not to. Barry had done so; between them they might come to different conclusions. 'I loved my sister. We didn't see each other overmuch the last few years, but it didn't seem to matter with us. She was happy with Clive, I didn't want to queer their pitch, and I could hardly expect Clive to welcome me.'

Barry had asked if Ginny had ever offered him money.

'Yes. Oh, I see what you're getting at, you think I was blackmailing her, that I killed her for money. Well, I'll tell you something, Detective Swan, I never accepted it. They were small amounts, to her that is, fifty pounds, or a hundred. She never held my prison sentence against me, but there was no way I was going to give her the chance to think less of me.'

Harvey was now living in Ipswich. It had taken him some time to get his life together again and he had, as he told his former landlady, moved to be nearer his sister. 'It wasn't easy getting a job, a tax-paying job, that is, but Charles was wonderful. He knew what I'd been and said he was prepared to take a chance. Only one chance. He knew I had an eye for antiques but told me if anything went missing I was out and he would not hesitate to call the police. That was seven years ago. I've been there ever since. I live over the shop now.'

'If he does a bit of buying he has access to a van,' Ian said, 'so he's another one we can't rule out altogether.'

But by the early evening they knew that, although Harvey had no alibi for the time when Debbie Orchard was murdered, he was in the shop when his sister was. Charles Matthews said they were both there to receive a delivery. The delivery firm, one which they used frequently, confirmed they had arrived outside the Ipswich shop at two and had not left until almost four because it was their last drop and they had stayed for a cup of tea. They had even faxed through a copy of the delivery note. But still they dared not rule him out.

Things were slowly beginning to move. Ian had a quick drink then went home to wait for Moira.

5

Every man available had been seconded to help with the double murder inquiry; everyone known to the victims had to be questioned, but so far they all appeared to be above suspicion. A team of detectives was systematically calling on every business in the area which provided any sort of delivery service: postmen, milkmen, florists, taxi firms, laundry firms, grocers, the list was endless. This had to be done because husbands could not always be relied upon to be *au fait* with the running of a home.

The optimism of the previous day had disappeared by the time Ian got home that night although Moira was pleased he had not stopped off on the way.

'I always do,' she said when he reminded her to keep the chain in place if he was not at home. 'Any news?'

'Not really.' He was determined to keep off the subject of the murders. The atmosphere was a little less strained at number 14 but there was still some work to do on his marriage. 'Do you want a hand with that?' He pointed to the chopping board upon which salad vegetables lay waiting to be prepared to accompany the chilli and pitta bread Moira said they were having.

'Yes, please.'

Ian picked up a knife and set to. The outcome, when it was assembled in a bowl, was not exactly elegant but it was colourful. 'By the way, how's John Freeling?'

Moira stared at him. He really was making an effort. 'He's fine now Mary's back. She returned the very night we were having a drink, worried sick, apparently, that he'd done something daft.'

'How come?' Ian took a radish from the bowl and crunched it.

'John had left the lights on when he came into the office that morning, probably his mind was elsewhere, so when Mary came back during the afternoon and found them on and the house empty she thought he'd gone out somewhere the previous night and not returned. To complicate matters, when she rang the office whoever took the call didn't know the situation and just said John wasn't in without explaining he was out on site. After work John and I went straight to the pub but by that time she'd panicked and contacted the police. He was so relieved to know she cared that much. I think they'll be all right, as long as he doesn't let things slip again.' Ian took the hint.

Moira tipped a tin of kidney beans into the mince mixture; when she stopped stirring, the steam, no longer being dispersed, rose in a cloud and settled around her head. 'My God, Ian!'

'What?'

'It's just occurred to me, you've been saying about not letting anyone in, but supposing it was the police?'

He closed his eyes. No, he said silently, please, anything but that.

'Where're you going?'

'I won't be a minute, I just want to make a phone call.' He did so and, much as he would have liked to go back to find out what results it produced, remained at home to share a meal with his wife. He tried not to think about what she had suggested. That night was the first since the row that she did not keep a space between them in the bed.

The fear that she might be right had turned into a certainty by the time he listened to what Markham had to say.

'Mrs Baxter made a 999 call about four months ago. Her

husband says he knows nothing about it. He suspects she didn't want to alarm him. He was away at the time and she was convinced there was someone prowling around outside. A patrol car responded in . . .' Markham checked his notes, 'nine minutes, but they didn't find anyone. From the report it looks as if either the security lights frightened someone off or maybe an animal activated them. There's no way out except via the lane and, realistically, you'd need a car if you intended breaking in and getting away with it.'

Ian sighed. One of their own men? Was it possible? Yes, it was. Mrs Baxter summoned help, she would remember the officer who came to her assistance – how easy for him to return, to say he needed to ask a few more questions on some pretext or another. It might not even have been the officers themselves. It could be the co-ordinator. Ian had heard enough locker-room talk to know the word could have been passed on, something along the lines of a good-looking woman like that, out there all alone.

'Which officers responded?'

'PCs Stone and Jackson,' Markham said.

Never in a million years, Ian told himself. Not those two. They were solid, hard-working men, long partnered and reliable. But still he had to ask them.

'All right, Markham, we know the Orchards didn't make an emergency call during the last couple of months – go back further, a year, say.' Stone and Jackson were not on duty that morning. Because Ian did not believe they were in any way responsible he decided to wait until they came in to question them.

Barry was equally despondent when he learned of the latest angle. His views on the culpability of Stone and Jackson matched the Chief's but there were other officers and other possibilities which were being checked. It need not necessarily have been an emergency call; one or both of the women might have lost something or handed something in. There were many other reasons for contacting the police apart from an emergency.

Barry went to the canteen for coffee. The day had passed and they were no further ahead except that a few more lab reports had been returned. Despondency was setting in. Outside, the sky was beginning to darken, street lights emphasising the gloom. Ian stood in the window and watched the pedestrians on the opposite side of the road. There were women with shopping and children, teenagers in small groups and a few men. Any one of those women might be the next victim. It was a thought he immediately stifled. There must not be a next one.

Sensing the Chief's mood, Barry had also purchased a slice of fruit cake. Food always made him happier. Ian was wiping his fingers on a paper serviette when DC Campbell came up to announce that neither of the Orchards had contacted the police for any reason during the past eighteen months. In a way it was a relief. It was also another setback.

'Look, your theory about the similarities. There's one we haven't looked into.'

'What's that?'

Barry took out a packet of cigarettes. Strictly speaking they were not supposed to smoke here but Ian was the most senior officer in the building at that moment so the rules could be bent. 'I know a lot of people decide to wait to have children these days, but Mrs Orchard was twenty-nine, Ginny Baxter thirty. And her husband's no youngster.'

Ian resented this oblique reminder of the discrepancy between his own and Moira's age. 'Well, go on.'

'Would it have shown up during the PM if they *couldn't* have children?'

'No, not necessarily.' Ian toyed thoughtfully with a biro. A doctor would know a lot about his patients' lifestyles – a family doctor, one in whom they might confide, even more. And he would have the necessary anatomical knowledge to strangle someone quickly. Or a specialist. Why not? He would have personal details. A female perpetrator had virtually been ruled out. Debbie Orchard was fit and strong, Virginia

69

Baxter was tall, and they had been easily overpowered with no signs of a struggle.

'Let's see the files again. A lot of women choose women doctors, especially if there're gynaecological problems.'

Barry shook his head. 'The Orchards were with the Waveney Road Health Centre. You never get the same doctor twice in a row there, and the Baxters were with Dan Langdon's lot.'

'I know Dan, I'll speak to him myself.' Dan was a family man, pictures of his four children were pinned to the wall and stood in frames on his desk. Ian thought him an unlikely candidate but before such judgements were made they needed to know the answer to a question.

Dan Langdon was out on house calls. Ian said he would try him again later. Meanwhile he despatched Barry to the Waveney Road Health Centre while he awaited the arrival of PCs Stone and Jackson.

Frank Stone was what the Chief described as one of the old school yet he had adapted readily to change. He was getting on for retirement but was not, unlike a few of his colleagues, prepared to spend the time counting the days and doing as little as possible; he was dreading rather than anticipating the point when he would begin drawing his pension. He was able to recall, with little reference to his notebook, the visit to the house in Broomhill Lane.

'We put it down to the lady being nervous on her own, sir,' he said. 'And we didn't pass another car or a pedestrian – out there at that time of night they'd've been noticeable.'

Ian did not ask whether he had later made any comments about Mrs Baxter's appearance. PC Stone would not have done so.

Peter Jackson was a younger man but it was difficult to tell whether he had been produced in the same mould as his partner or whether his attitude had been acquired by osmosis. He was indignant at the suggestion that he might have spoken lewdly about Mrs Baxter. 'I never discuss women in that way, sir,' he said, staring at a spot somewhere above Ian's head. And the co-ordinator on duty that night was a dark-haired, rosy-cheeked young lady appropriately named Belle Foster.

Barry Swan returned from the surgery in a disgruntled mood. The receptionist had been less than helpful and he had been made to wait before anyone would see him. He had gone back to the desk and, in a loud voice, made it clear a second time who he was. She obviously did not want his sort hanging around the waiting-room as this produced a result. The doctor's manner was hardly conducive to cheering up patients if he spoke to them as he did to Barry; having given him a lecture on patient confidentiality, he finally agreed to press a few keys on the computer terminal on his desk and check Debbie Orchard's records. Doc Harris would have had a fit; here no individual was known to any practitioner and the patients took their chance as to whom they were seen by.

Deborah Jean Orchard had a clean bill of health and had never discussed the possibility of infertility. Neither had her husband.

Ian met with the same response but Dan Langdon was prepared to give him the information over the telephone and suggested they got together for a drink one evening. Ian went to give Superintendent Thorne an update still feeling that their childless state bore some relevance.

'I shan't be much more than an hour,' Moira said as she picked up a couple of bulging black bin-liners. 'But I did promise Deirdre I'd get this stuff to her this evening.'

'Shall I come with you?'

'Whatever for?'

'You're loaded.'

'No need, I can manage.' She picked up a smaller bag, smiling secretly. He was still on his toes. It would not surprise her if he rang up on some feeble pretext whilst she was at Deirdre's to check that she was there. It was good while it lasted. 'I'll get a take-away, shall I?'

Ian switched on the television. Deep down he trusted Moira, but just because nothing had happened this time did not mean it never would. He was capable of dividing his thoughts, part of which were on Moira, part on the inanity of the sit-com he was watching, and part on the murdered women. Whatever he had said on that awful night when he came across Moira and John Freeling, he was incapable of physically hurting her. So how was it that two women had inspired enough loathing for someone to kill them, someone, apparently, who was not even close to them? The nagging question was still at the forefront: what if there was no connection? They would have wasted so much time and effort looking for the wrong things and the longer a case continued, the less likely the chance of success. Superintendent Thorne had been his usual supportive self and had opined that the incidents were almost too random. Despite the similarities there was an element of confusion. Hardest of all to believe was that the backgrounds of the victims were almost unimpeachable. DC Campbell had worked hard on their earlier years. Debbie had left school and gone straight to teacher-training college, Ginny had dropped out for a year and done the student trek across Europe in a van before going to university. Both had had boyfriends, but not many, before they married and Ginny had lived with a fellow hippie-type before returning to the bosom of her family and getting a good degree. At a gathering at her parents' house she met Clive, a divorcee, and was instantly attracted to him. Clive, recovering from a marriage where every word he uttered was analysed and found wanting, fell in love with Ginny's straightforward simplicity and gentle ways. There was nothing in either background to augur their tragic futures.

The commercial break began and Ian wondered why the adverts were always so much louder than the programmes. Perhaps it was so you could hear from the kitchen when you rushed off to make a cup of tea. The front door crashed. He grimaced. How long had he been saying he would plane a bit off the side? Once it dried out he forgot about it again.

'Yes, in here on our knees,' he called out in response to Moira's question as to where he wanted to eat.

He was restless that night, sleeping fitfully, unable to see that Moira had presented him with half a clue, but he had overlooked one vital point.

'I can't put my finger on it. It's not that we're not doing everything possible, there's just no substance to it.' Ian rubbed his chin. He had made the mistake of shaving the previous night, he was going to look scruffy by the end of the day. 'There's no feel, nothing tangible.'

Barry knew what he meant. Despite technology, instinct still existed, a sense of knowing when you were going in the right direction. This time there was a flatness.

'And I don't feel I know the victims, and what makes it worse is I can't accuse anyone of not doing their homework. Look at this, for example.' He thrust a couple of sheets of neatly typed paper across the desk. 'You can't get a more comprehensive report than that.' He screwed up his eyes to read, upside-down, who was responsible. He was amazed. It was Markham. 'But I still don't know what makes these people tick. And there isn't a whiff of scandal. All right, before you say it, I know we tend to forget the majority are law-abiding citizens, but that's the whole point, they don't come to our attention.'

'I agree. And what's the motive?' There always was one, no matter how incomprehensible it might appear to others.

Ian stood up and grabbed his jacket which was draped over the back of his chair. 'I'm going out.'

He left the building, ignoring the blue sky and the crispness of the day. Shoots of bulbs were now an inch or so high in the raised beds around the entrance and already the tiny sprigs of new leaves were clustered around the pruned stems of the rose bushes. All he saw was the empty lager can which rattled erratically across the tarmac.

73

He drove into the car-park of the comprehensive school. The main building was immense and soulless, consisting of squares of glass and rectangles of concrete and peeling paint. Scattered around were other buildings, similar but on a smaller scale. No doubt they housed the science labs and cookery departments. Beyond the chain link fence were the playing fields, marked out now for football and hockey; the playing fields where Debbie Orchard had spent a large percentage of her short life. Seeing where she actually worked brought home to him the waste.

Mark had been a pupil here but Ian had only been to the school on a couple of occasions. Mostly it had been down to Moira to attend open evenings and school plays. Having no idea of whom he wanted to see or what he was going to ask, he headed towards the large porch of the main building. Inside, it was warm. Just as police stations have an aroma peculiar to them all, so do schools: it was a smell which could not be broken down into components but one which had lingered on Mark long after he had walked home each day.

In the corridor he was swallowed up by a crowd of noisy thirteen-year-olds as they made their way to another classroom, files and books under their arms, their uniforms adapted to their own tastes. They made no concession to his age or to the fact that he was a visitor and he struggled not to reprimand them as he was jostled. There were notices with arrows on the wall ahead, one of which directed him to the office. 'Please knock and enter', it said on the door. He did so.

The woman behind the desk was Ian's idea of a middle-aged spinster – not that he could have guessed her age with any accuracy, it was just a look she had, a settled complacency, and the manner in which she dressed as if she was now content to drift placidly on, expecting nothing. As if her aid to sight was an impediment to speech, she removed her glasses before saying, 'Good morning, can I help you?' Her tone was friendly.

'I'm not really sure.' Ian introduced himself, producing his identity. The woman leaned forward. She smiled. 'I'd never

74

seen one before, you know. I always wondered what they looked like. Still, I'm not sure I'd know the real thing if I saw another.' Ian had given up on the idea that the killer might be a police officer, but he was aware how easy it was to hire a uniform from a fancy dress place and make up some bogus identification. The hire shops were being checked. 'I'm so sorry, please have a seat. Is it one of the children you've come about?' She shook her head in mock despair. 'They're all right really. Most of them. But you know what it's like these days, we've got a couple of little devils.' She blushed rather charmingly. 'Well, of course you know what it's like.'

'Not one of the children, no. I'm here because of Mrs Orchard.'

'Forgive me, I made it sound as if I'd forgotten about her already. So many policemen have been here recently I thought they had finished with us.'

'You were interviewed yourself, Mrs . . .' He had noticed the wedding ring. Her face hardened for a second. Seeing the direction of his glance she looked at it herself.

'Prior. Evelyn Prior. I'm divorced. Yes, I was asked some questions, if that's what you mean by being interviewed.'

'May I ask you a couple more now?'

'Of course.' She seemed pleased and sat back in the chair as if preparing herself for a treat.

'Do you know all the staff here?'

'It depends what you mean by know. I know them all by name and the subjects they teach, and I keep a rota of where they are at any given moment during the day. In a place this size and with so many of them it makes life more simple. There are half a dozen I know really well and some moderately so.'

'And where would you place Mrs Orchard?'

'I . . .' She hesitated. 'I know Roy better.'

'That wasn't what I asked,' Ian pointed out gently.

Her expression was defiant. 'I knew Debbie and I always found her pleasant.' Ian waited. 'I know I shouldn't say this, she's dead, but there were times I got the impression she

75

didn't have much patience with those she believed to be incompetent.' She bit her lip. 'Perhaps I'm being unfair. It was only one incident, and I can assure you it has no bearing upon her death. She was very cruel to me on one occasion. I had made a mistake, oh, it was definitely my mistake, and a very stupid one. I admitted it and apologised. It was to do with a booking for transport for a tennis match and I got the time wrong. She was furious – well, it's understandable really, the girls were nervous anyway, and then the coach didn't turn up. She called me a menopausal old hag.' Evelyn Prior blushed again. This time it was not so becoming.

'At last,' Ian said.

'Pardon?'

'Nothing.' But there was a faint smile on his lips. 'And that was the end of the incident?'

'More or less. She went to the headmaster but he didn't take the matter up. You see, I had only heard that morning that my sister had cancer, I wasn't concentrating on work.'

'You've been more than helpful, Mrs Prior. Thank you. Now I'd like to speak to one or two of the teaching staff if it's possible. Do you think you could check with the headmaster for me?'

'He would like to see you first,' she said when she replaced the receiver, and she told him where he could find him.

At last, Ian thought again as he climbed the stairs. Debbie Orchard, although dead, was beginning to come to life for him. She had faults like anyone else.

Phillip Havers tried to be intimidating but failed. For a start he was not expecting someone of Ian's height to loom over his desk. 'I'd prefer it if you questioned the staff in their own time,' he said. 'Things have been disrupted enough here as it is. And with Mr Orchard on compassionate leave we're two teachers short. And all the gossip and speculation that's flying around does neither the reputation of the school nor the pupils any good.'

Ian noted the order of priority. 'In that case, the sooner I

76

speak to them, the better. The alternative is to bring them into the station. I have no intention of interrupting classes, at this point, but I cannot see what harm it would do to talk to those with a free period.'

Phillip Havers, realising he had been outwitted, had no choice but to agree.

There were only three people in the staff-room; two were female, one of whom sat unnecessarily close to her male colleague. A quaintly old-fashioned thought came to mind as Ian watched them. They had, he decided, been canoodling. Twenty minutes later he had learned nothing new, except, as if in counterpoint to what Evelyn Prior told him, that Debbie had once spent four hours of her own time in Rickenham General casualty department with a female student who had injured herself on the sports field and then insisted upon staying with her until her parents returned in the evening. 'She wasn't a latch-key kid, or anything. She was sixteen and her parents were expected back about nine, it was just that the girl was so upset because she wouldn't be able to compete in the county athletics trials.'

The exercise had been interesting but not illuminating; it had, however, provided Ian with what he was after, a 'feel' for the case. For some reason his mood lifted. Tomorrow he might do a spot more interviewing himself.

'The Assistant Chief Constable wants a word with you,' were DS Swan's first words of greeting.

'Does he now?' Ian sighed. Why was it that the only time the brass wanted a word in your ear was when you were off duty, somewhere you ought not to be, or bending the rules?

'Well?'

Ian had made the call in private. It was typical of Barry to want to know the details.

'In a nutshell, he doesn't want a third murder and begrudgingly he has offered us a couple more men.' He did not add that the ACC had been less than complimentary about their performance so far.

'Better late than never, I suppose.' But they were both thinking the same thing: what use was more manpower when they were already doing everything possible?

They were in the general office, a large, open-plan area from which the detectives worked from their own desks. The morning's briefing was over, the major crimes dealt with first. Even the irrepressible DC Emmanuel was subdued; lack of progress was beginning to affect them all. The telephone rang once or twice but calls connected to the case went straight through to the control room. A few more lab results had trickled in and many false leads were being eliminated.

Both inquests were out of the way; as predicted, they had gone without a hitch and Debbie Orchard had already been cremated. Ginny Baxter's funeral would take place in a couple of days' time. And out there was a killer, one who knew enough not to leave any traces, one who knew how to kill quickly and cleanly and who might well get away with it. A sound escaped the Chief's lips: it was a splutter of disgust.

Doc Harris was in the reception area when Ian crossed it on his way to the control room. 'Ah, Ian. Had to take a look at some young tearaway who got into a scrap at the bus station. No serious damage. Fancy a drink later or is Moira expecting you?'

'Why not? Give me a ring later.' He deserved it. He had, after all, been going straight home lately.

Ian picked up a long list of all the businesses who operated a delivery service. There were ticks against many of them but still a lot to go. Unfortunately they did not all keep accurate records. It would be at least another day before they would know the outcome.

The bright, sunny sky beckoned. After weeks, even months of rain Ian wanted to be outside. He left a message as to where he could be found and decided everyone else could get on with the routine.

Turning right out of the car-park he was soon at the top of

the High Street. He crossed the bridge and within a minute or so the town was behind him. The branches of trees on the narrow road met overhead and entwined. At this time of year the sky was visible through them; in the summer the road was a cool, green avenue. He entered Broomhill Lane. The first house was, as Baxter had said, empty, purchased as a holiday home. Next came the farm, which appeared deserted although Pete Morris was probably somewhere about on his tractor. Ian had no intention of tramping over the still-sodden fields to find him. There was no reply when he rang the door bell; Mrs Morris and the children had gone into town. The next property was the scene of the murder, the windows blank against the winter sun.

He pulled into the grass verge, leaving enough room for other traffic to pass, and went up the path to the Connors' bungalow. Albert was a grizzled old man, his back humped, a walking frame beside his chair. Because of constant pain his expression was fierce but his manner was not. His wife was chirpy and plump and explained that they did not go out much but that neither of them had seen or heard anything on that fatal day or the days leading up to it. Ian left after only a few minutes. They were, he sensed, the kind of people who would not hold back if they knew anything or make something up if they didn't.

The last house belonged to Tom and Jean Marsh and its proportions had been ruined. The original stone was all that had not been tampered with. The sash windows had been replaced by mullioned bay ones; the door was now double-glazed with frosted glass, and artificial carriage lamps were mounted on either side of it. Baxter, Ian recalled, had described the Marshes as common. When he met them, although no snob himself, Ian found he had to agree.

Tom Marsh answered the door, a drink in his hand. He wore a loud jacket and a gaudy cravat tucked into the neck of a white shirt. He was overfed and porcine, his eyes no more than slits in folds of flesh. In the drive were three expensive models of car, material proof of their financial status but unsuitable for the country roads and a county with no motorway. The money, Ian decided, must be inherited. Baxter had told them that neither of the Marshes worked.

'We're having a drink to celebrate my wife's birthday,' Marsh said, 'and a couple of our friends are here. You people have been trampling about the place for ages. I'm sure this isn't necessary.'

'It is necessary, Mr Marsh.' Ian was needled by the man's attitude. He would use the old cherry, it rarely failed. 'But if it's more convenient we can talk in my office.' It did not fail this time.

'You'd better come in then. But I'm warning you, if this spoils my wife's do I shall have words with the Chief Constable. He's a friend of one of my partners.'

'Partners?' Marsh did work then.

'I'm semi-retired. I hold a consultancy position with a financial advisory company.'

The Chief Constable, Ian thought as he followed Marsh into the house, could not spend a single minute on police business if everyone who claimed to have him as a friend or a friend of someone they knew was to be believed. The poor man must exist in a non-stop social whirl. He smiled pleasantly as he was shown into the kitchen.

From a room across the passage he heard the chink of glasses and the murmur of conversation. The interior decoration matched that of the outside – it was vulgar; gilt, wrought iron and mirrors predominated in the hall but were not out of place with the puce wallpaper and carpet. The kitchen was equipped with every appliance imaginable but did not look as if it got much use. On the worktop were the packets and trays from which the buffet lunch had originated.

'Oh, I thought it was another guest,' a plummy voice announced from the doorway. The woman, presumably Jean Marsh, was wearing chiffon, which Ian thought a little over the top for a lunchtime, and puce was obviously her favourite colour. He had to admit it did enhance her dark looks. She was one of the few women who could get away with it. She, too, had a glass in her hand but Ian was not offered any refreshment. He would have liked to have been, simply in order to be able to refuse.

With his wife's appearance Marsh's attitude softened. 'We didn't really know them,' he said, referring to the Baxters, 'they were private people. I don't think they had many guests at all, and they certainly never invited us in for a neighbourly drink. Not like us, eh, love? Nothing like a good party, that's what we always say. Mind, we've only two other couples here at the moment, we're saving ourselves for the big celebration tonight.'

Jean Marsh had been shopping in Ipswich on the day of the murder. She had, during her initial interview, voluntarily produced credit card slips to prove it. Her husband had been playing golf at the Country Club and had stayed drinking in the evening, an alibi which was soon confirmed. They had nothing further to add. Ian was about to leave when a third person entered the kitchen. This time it was a sour-faced youth, as dark-haired as Mrs Marsh. The downward turn of his mouth and his general demeanour suggested a spoilt only child, which was exactly what he was.

'This is my son, Damien,' Marsh said, placing an arm across his shoulders which caused his jacket to strain at the seams. 'Chief Inspector Roper.' At least Marsh had the manners to introduce them; Damien did not have the manners to respond at all. He was silent.

'Were you here on the day Mrs Baxter was murdered?' Ian mentally ran down the list. He was sure that name wasn't on it.

'No. He was staying with friends for a couple of weeks.' It was his mother who answered. 'He came back especially for my birthday. Wasn't that sweet?' Damien pulled away when she planted a small kiss on his cheek. Ian wondered if the boy was dumb. Baxter had said he thought he was about eighteen. It was term time – presumably he had left school if he was staying with friends, and, presumably, he was unemployed.

'Do you work, Damien?'

'No.'

'It's very difficult for him. He didn't do all that well at school, he can't concentrate on things for very long, his mind's just too quick, you see.' Jean Marsh was a mother who had decided to make a virtue out of her son's short attention span, perhaps because she was partly responsible for it. No doubt he had been inundated with all the latest electronic equipment since he was a small child but Ian bet books had never been on his Christmas present list. But he was not here to judge.

'Where did you go to school, Damien?'

'Rickenham.'

'The comprehensive? My son went there.' Something more than monosyllabic answers would have been welcome. It crossed his mind that Mark may have known the boy.

'Yeah. I left three years ago.'

Jackpot. Not only had Damien spoken a whole sentence, he must have known, or been aware of the existence of, both Roy and Debbie Orchard even if neither of them had been responsible for his education. He did. 'Yeah, he taught me English. He was all right.'

'And Mrs Orchard?'

Damien shook his head.

Ian wished Jean Marsh a happy birthday and went back to the car. There was no reason for anyone to have contacted Damien Marsh. He had left the school three years ago and was away at the time of the murders. Why then had his parents exchanged that nervous glance when he asked if the boy knew Mrs Orchard? And how did he live? Surely his parents were not content to hand him out money to supplement whatever benefits he might be drawing. It was possible, of course, that Damien was also in possession of some kind of inheritance. It might be worth investigating.

'I told you, Barry, once we'd found one connection we'd find others.'

'Yes, but there are over a thousand pupils at the school now, let alone how many have passed through since the Orchards began teaching there.'

'But how many of them live next door to the Baxters?'

'He was away at the time .'

'He was not staying in his parents' house.' Ian was mentally kicking himself. He should have asked the exact whereabouts of Damien at the time.

'If there's anything to find, Alan'll find it.'

'I know. I'm meeting Doc Harris at seven, fancy a pint?'

'Not tonight. Lucy's doing a special meal.'

Gone were the days when Barry could be counted on as a drinking partner, when any excuse sufficed to prevent him returning to his empty flat. Even when he had a woman lined up he always found time for a quick drink first.

The Doc was waiting downstairs. 'This is a bit of luck. I can push the boat out tonight because I won't be using the car tomorrow. Got a locum covering for me because I've got to attend some goddamn seminar on paediatrics up at Rickenham General. I can't understand the modern world, all these bloody forums and discussions and what I believe they call sharing of ideas – it's futile, and if you ask me, it's just an excuse for the NHS to employ more bodies. If I can't recognise a case of mumps or measles or meningitis by now I might as well call it a day. Listen to me, you've got enough on your plate without my whining.'

They were half-way up the High Street, their footsteps taking them both in the direction of the Crown which was also the Doc's favourite pub next to the Country Club. He lived in a detached house in Maple Avenue, one of the better parts of the town but within walking distance of the shops. There was no juke-box in the Crown and the only fruit machine was stuck away in the flagstoned corridor leading to the toilets. There was also an open fire at each end which made it too hot when it was busy.

On the other side of the road was a group of teenagers waiting to go in to see the latest Sylvester Stallone film. At least, Ian thought, they were doing something other than hanging around making a nuisance of themselves.

'Shirley's out tonight,' the Doc continued as the warmth of

the Crown hit them. 'My first entirely free night for ages and she's already made other arrangements. Some brass band concert or similar. Not my cup of tea, give me jazz any time.'

Each with a pint of Adnams, the Doc's in a glass with a handle, they settled down somewhere between the two fires. The room was full of the smoky scent of apple wood. Ian abstemiously watched Doc Harris as he demolished a plate of homemade steak and onion pie with chips and peas. Cholesterol held no fears for him. At nine he left a disappointed friend and went home. He and Moira were discussing the events of their respective days when the telephone rang. It was Mark. Moira rang him back as he was in a call box. Satisfied that their son was healthy and enjoying himself, they had a small brandy each and went to bed.

6

Marian Thomas was losing her nerve. She wished she had a telephone number or knew where he lived, it would have been so much easier to ring or drop a note through the door telling him not to come. He frightened her, she realised, and she had bought herself a bottle of wine to drink after she had told him it was over. He might, of course, be as relieved as herself for she had no idea how he really felt about her.

The double chime of the bell of her modern, terraced house made her jump although she was expecting it. When she opened the door and saw how hard it was raining, it was impossible to leave him standing there. His hair was sparkling with droplets and the shoulders of his jacket were wet. He smiled as he stepped into the hall and pushed open the lounge door.

'Look, I don't quite know how to say this,' she began, wringing her hands nervously.

'Say what?' His smile was unpleasant, which she had not noticed before.

'I've been thinking, and ... well, please believe me, it's nothing to do with you, I've enjoyed your company, the thing is, I still love my husband.' It was out, she began to relax. Then, when he prodded her with his forefinger, pushing her further into the room, what had been a vague fear turned into terror.

'Nobody dumps me, do you hear? What's your game, you little bitch? Just fancied a few free drinks, did you?'

It was so unfair, she had bought her share too, but he was

not in the mood to be argued with and she saw how easily he was provoked. 'No, I – ' but he was not prepared to hear whatever she was about to say.

Something happened to her as she thought that Jim had never hurt her, not even verbally, not until the end when he said he couldn't live with her any more. This room, a little shabby because some of the furniture was second-hand, had been furnished lovingly between them. This man was defiling it with his presence. It made her angry.

'I want you to leave,' she said coldly. 'Right now. I will not be treated like this in my own home.'

'Do you now? And supposing I don't want to go?'

'Get out. I'm calling the police.' She turned to where the telephone rested on the sideboard but she was not fast enough. Wrongly, in her naïvety, she had assumed these words were enough to frighten anybody. The receiver was wrenched from her hand and the plug ripped from its socket. 'I don't think so. You'll pay for this, you bitch.' With the first stinging blow she staggered against the sideboard, the bottles of drink left over from Christmas clanking inside. A bolt of pain shot up her spine as it connected with the corner. The second blow sent her to the floor where she crouched, waiting for the inevitable. And then he stopped because several things had gone through his mind.

Quite gently, he took her arm and pulled her to her feet. It choked him to have to apologise to a woman, but he had to. He said he was desperate and hurt, that he hadn't wanted it to finish but now he realised she would never want to see him again. 'I'll go. I really am sorry, Marian. Please don't hold it against me. Perhaps one day . . .' He left the sentence unfinished. There would be no one day, he would make sure of that.

Immediately he had gone she shut the door and bolted it, leaning against it for several minutes to get her breath back. Then panic overtook her: supposing he had not really gone but was waiting to catch her by surprise? She ran to the kitchen and checked the back door, pulling the blinds down over the windows before running upstairs to make sure all the windows were locked, although she knew they had not been open for weeks. She repeated it all a second time before she was satisfied then opened the fridge, adrenalin making her heavy-handed. It tilted forward slightly, the contents juddering, but nothing was spilled. With shaking hands she managed to extract the cork from the bottle and poured some wine, a few drops splashing to the floor. The misted bottle was slippery: she placed it on the draining board before she spilled that too. The cooker clock said eight thirty-five. Impossible to imagine so little time had passed since that ring on the bell.

The small lamp on the sideboard had overturned. She straightened it, pushed the telephone cable back into its socket and sat down with her glass of wine.

When her heartbeat had slowed sufficiently and her breathing was easier she picked up the receiver and dialled Jim's number.

'Oh, no, not again.' Moira was filling the kettle at the sink when the sky darkened and the first, large drops of rain hit the window. 'I think it's sleet.'

'I'll drop you off in that case.' Mark was in possession of their second car so Moira usually walked as she enjoyed the exercise. Occasionally, if their hours coincided, Ian gave her a lift. She could have had his car at any time because he could always use a police vehicle, but she was afraid of becoming lazy.

Outside John Freeling's premises Ian watched as Moira struggled with her umbrella, which was immediately blown inside out. She shrugged and waved and ran towards the entrance.

'Neither Jason Proctor nor his father has a record,' Alan Campbell said before going to find out if any villain with a predilection for GBH or ABH had recently been released although the form did not fit anyone from their patch. The only likely candidate had another seven years to serve. Ian decided he would go and speak to Roy Orchard, ask him what he knew about Damien Marsh. He had to consult a map to remind himself of the road in which Orchard's parents lived but only because there was a Deben Lane, Close, Road and Avenue in that area and he always forgot which was which. They were so called because the stream that flowed through the north side of Rickenham Green was a tributary of the river Deben and, back in the sixties when the building trade was flourishing, many of the roads required to service the new houses were named after Suffolk rivers.

The house he approached had weathered nicely and was well constructed, if a little too square. It was semi-detached and had a general appearance of neatness; the flower beds were tidy, the windows clean. The door was opened by an exhausted-looking woman in an apron.

'Hello. I see it's stopped at last,' she said, glancing at the dismal sky. 'At least we were spared snow this winter.' She was speaking automatically, making the right noises, and Ian guessed she was struggling to cope. Her daughter-in-law had been murdered and her inconsolable son was temporarily living with her. 'It's Roy you've come to see, I expect. He's upstairs, I'll get him.'

'Not yet. I'd like a word or two with you first.'

She nodded and ushered him down the short passage to the kitchen, where she turned the gas down under a pan. 'Please excuse the mess,' she said.

People always made an excuse for the process of everyday living, yet meals had to be prepared, beds were slept in and rooms became untidy.

'How well did you know Debbie?' Ian asked. They were perched on two stools by a section of a worktop. There was no kitchen table or room to put one. Presumably there was a dining-room. He could not help observing such things even as he listened to Roy's mother. Gradually she began to relax.

It was a relief to her to speak to an outsider because natural conversation in her house was impossible at the moment.

Mrs Orchard had liked Debbie. She was about to produce some photographs when there were footsteps on the stairs. Roy Orchard pushed open the door. His face was as pale as when Ian had last seen him and he had lost weight. There were lines creasing his brow and running from the outer corners of his nose to his mouth which had not been there before his wife's death.

'Inspector Roper, isn't it?'

Ian did not correct him; he was surprised he could remember anything concerning their previous meetings. 'Mr Orchard, do you recall a pupil named Damien Marsh?'

'Damien? What's he got to do with it?'

'Not necessarily anything.'

'He was hopeless. One of those boys you know your efforts are wasted on. When he did turn up he didn't pay attention. I know respect is a dated concept these days, but he was one of the few I'd like to have slapped.'

'Did you know his parents?'

'Yes. Unfortunately they had the attitude that Damien's problems were the fault of the school but I got the impression he ruled the roost at home. They threw money at him, no wonder he got in with the wrong crowd.'

'The wrong crowd? Was he in trouble?'

'Now and again. What's – ' but Roy's question was interrupted by Ian's bleeper going off.

'May I use your telephone?'

Mrs Orchard nodded. There was one on the wall near the fridge. His stomach constricted as he listened.

'I have to go, I'm needed back at the station. I hope you don't think me rude rushing away.'

He was shown to the door. Roy remained in the kitchen as if moving was too much of an effort.

It mightn't mean anything, he told himself as he reversed the car and pointed it in the direction of the town. Just because a girl has not turned up for work and isn't answering her telephone does not mean she is dead. But the fear remained with him, instinct told him she was. He tried to rationalise the situation. She'd taken an illicit day off to go shopping; she was hung-over and had unplugged the telephone; she had simply overslept. But if this girl was unreliable her employer would not have troubled the police unless, thanks to the awareness of the recent dangers, she was being over-cautious. If the publicity was working it would not matter that their time was being wasted. Anything was better than another victim.

'Someone's over there, or should be by now,' Barry Swan told him when he hurried into the control room. 'I thought you'd want to know. Mrs Franks insisted she wasn't that sort of girl, that she would have contacted her if she wasn't coming in and that she had never taken a day off she wasn't entitled to.'

One of the control room telephones rang. Barry and Ian stood motionless and silent while someone else answered it.

'Sir, that was PC Becks. We've got another one.'

No words were exchanged as DS Swan and DCI Roper made their way towards Waveney Road. In mockery of someone else's tragedy the clouds were swept away in a brisk wind and the street was bathed in sunlight which was reflected in the puddles rapidly drying in the gutters. It was needless to use the warning light which could be magnetically attached to the roof of the car, it was too late for Carrie Griffiths. They turned right at the Station Arms, or what had once been that hotel. On the demolition list for years, it was now boarded up against squatters and the landlady, Gloria, had finally given up and gone to Ireland to be with her dead husband's family. In reality the building looked no worse than when it had been a going concern. Two more streets of terraced housing before they emerged into what Ian described as the wastelands, where small blocks of flats faced each other around scrubby areas of grass, where there was always petty crime, where homes were considered as nothing more than a place to sleep at night, where neglect and despair went hand in hand. Magnolia House. A ridiculous name. To Ian it conjured up a family home of soft-coloured stone set in its own grounds with shrubs and flowers in abundance, the tree after which the house was named in the middle of a lawn, its sensuous, velvet blossoms opening as a prelude to summer. There were no magnolias here and probably never had been, only a few ill-nurtured saplings, their lower branches snapped.

They parked behind a panda car but only one or two people glanced in their direction. They had seen it all before, a police presence here was not unusual. The main entrance doors were half steel, half reinforced glass lined with metal mesh, but someone had still managed to crack them. The ground floor smelled of urine and damp rubbish and the walls were defaced with graffiti. As always Ian took the stairs but in places like this it was unlikely the lift was operational.

'Sir.' The young PC outside Carrie Griffiths' flat saluted as best he could because in his arms was a struggling black and white cat which mewed piteously. 'It belongs to the victim, we weren't sure what to do with him.'

'Hold on to him for now.' It would be cruel to send it out into the street if it was not used to it, but it was not a good idea to leave it running about the flat destroying evidence, of which, Ian was sure, there would be no signs. There were no gawpers here, the third floor seemed to be deserted. The officer who waited just inside the door was PC Becks, a man unlikely to panic and who had done the right things as a matter of routine.

'The cat, sir, it was licking her face.' Becks had taken two strides into the room, checked the body for vital signs, picked up the cat and taken two strides back.

Ian made himself get an impression of the room. It opened straight off the corridor and was medium-sized and not very tidy, but it had not been ransacked. On a chair in a corner were some articles of female underclothing; a pair of tights, still holding the shape of the wearer, trailed to the floor. Further back, through an open door, he saw part of an unmade bed. Then he studied the victim, but from where he stood. John Cotton would be less than pleased if he went trampling all over the flat.

The girl was facing him. Her hair was blonde, but not naturally so, there was a darker line where it parted. She was pretty in a full-lipped, snub-nosed way even in death. The underclothes? And her looks? Was there a sexual motive this time? Probably not, because the straight skirt and ecru knitted top she was wearing did not look as if they had been disturbed, and her black, knitted tights were in place. If Mrs Franks had not been a conscientious employer it would have been Carrie Griffiths' husband who found her.

They waited while the rest of the team arrived in twos and threes, the photographers first with their bulky equipment. One immediately started videoing the scene. Doc Harris was not available, it was Peregrine Danvers who came instead. Ian had not liked him initially, believing him to be a supercilious young fool, but his arrogance had been caused by shyness which was now wearing off. He could never replace the Doc, the rotund, balding man whose eyes were full of humour and intelligence, but he was pleasant and efficient.

'Good,' John Cotton said when he saw the cat. 'We'll examine that, too. You never know. And look on the bright side, cats shed hairs.'

Barry Swan had remained in conversation with the young PC, who was able to tell him that when they arrived they had knocked but received no answer. 'We knocked again then tried the handle. The door wasn't locked.' If it had been they would have had to refer back to their superiors for instructions. Despite public belief, police officers do not have the authority to go around kicking doors in without a very good reason and a girl not turning up for work was not one of them.

Once the routine was under way Ian organised yet another squad for house-to-house inquiries. He did so from the car while Barry drove. He was going to see Mrs Franks himself. Although not a suspect she might have plenty to tell him. 'Drop me off then find Brian Griffiths.' They knew the name of Carrie's husband from Mrs Franks who had also said Brian would have phoned if Carrie was ill.

Heads turned as he entered the small hairdressing salon. Few men passed over its threshold because it was not a unisex premises. There were, he noticed, still some women who had their hair set in the old-fashioned way and sat under the driers in their rollers. He ignored the stares of the ladies, who were undergoing what appeared to him to be a form of torture, and turned to face the mirrored wall and the reflections of the clients watching him in it as their hair was being cut or blow-dried. He saw at once who was in charge.

'Mrs Franks?' A pair of violet eyes met his. The woman, certainly not far off fifty, was beautiful. Her cheekbones and jaw were perfectly structured and the small web of crow's feet did nothing to detract from her looks. Yet when she spoke she came across as ordinary, her accent local, her way of speaking unfussy. For some reason Ian had expected more; but if there had been more, Mrs Franks would not be working in a back-street hairdresser's in Rickenham Green, even if it was her own business. 'I'm Detective – '

'I think I know who you are. You'd better come out to the back.' Her face had paled. 'Justin, would you see to Margaret, please?' She placed a tailcomb on the work bench. 'I'm sorry, Margaret, but this is important. Justin'll deduct ten per cent off your bill.'

Justin simpered. With his tight black jeans and peach-coloured shirt, it did not take much guessing as to which direction the boy's sexual preferences lay.

Mrs Franks pulled back a curtain made from strips of plastic. 'It's not very comfortable but we're short on space.' There was a table, a few shelves containing the tins and bottles necessary to her trade and tea-making equipment. Ian accepted a cup of coffee. He had experienced what he was feeling now before, with men as well as women. Certain people exuded a soothing aura, as if they were gently stroking your brow. It happened with voices too, when all you wanted to do was let them carry on talking.

93

'He's a bloody good hairdresser,' she said, as though she had read Ian's earlier thoughts. 'But I won't be able to keep him, not on what I pay. He could do so much better and it would be a shame to hold him back. Sugar?'

'No thanks.'

Mrs Franks turned to face him while she waited for the kettle to boil. 'Carrie's dead, isn't she?' The question could no longer be avoided.

'Yes, she is.'

'The same as the others?'

'We don't know for certain yet.' But it would be.

'Yes.' She poured boiling water into the mugs and added milk; they left wet rings on the table because her hand had shaken. 'I knew it. I sensed it this morning when she didn't show up. Carrie's been with me for nearly five years and she's never had a day off. Only once was she late and she rang me at home at seven thirty in the morning to say she would be late because she'd broken a tooth. I knew when it got to ten and she hadn't called, and nor had Brian . . .'

Ian nodded and saw tears fill the violet eyes.

'I'm sorry.' She fumbled for a handkerchief and blew her nose loudly.

'Mrs Franks – '

'Please call me Eileen.'

'What time was Carrie due to start work?'

'Today, at ten, but she's always in a few minutes before that. Other days it's eight thirty. She starts late on Wednesdays because we do a late night, a third off the price between five and seven o'clock, and there's always a couple of customers who insist Carrie does their hair. And this morning Janice Peters had an appointment and she wouldn't miss that, she tips well. I can't take it in, really I can't. Brian, does he know yet?'

'Someone's been sent to find him.'

'He works for the council, on the dustcarts.'

That information might save time. Ian used his mobile phone and contacted the control room.

'He'll be devastated, they've been going out since their schooldays, except Carrie broke it off once, she said she wanted to live a bit before she got married. She saw one or two other fellows but she went back to Brian, they were so right for each other, you could tell that by watching them.'

And here it was again, the total confidence that the victim had been happily married. 'But no children?'

'No. They wanted to wait until they got themselves out of Magnolia House. She was determined not to bring a child up there. They were saving, that's why she didn't mind the long hours. She's a good hairdresser, not in Justin's class, but certainly good enough for here, and, like I said, she was punctual.'

'What about friends? Was she popular?'

'Yes, very. She was happy-go-lucky, nothing seemed to get her down, maybe because she comes from a fairly large family with not enough money.'

Ian's mind wandered briefly. Was it possible that Carrie had been killed sometime yesterday after she left work? Had her predisposition to enjoying life led her to go too far – had the ever-patient Brian been driven to murder her? He could not have failed to know about the other murders, it would be easy enough to copy them.

'She used to go out with a group of girls on a Friday while Brian played darts, friends from school they were, but not so much lately. I think she'd started going to the bingo with her mother instead. The only night she and Brian went out was Saturday. Like I said, they were saving.'

'Boyfriends?'

Eileen shook her head. 'Only a couple when they split up. The lads used to buzz around her like flies but she always kept them at arm's length. Oh, surely you don't mean recently?'

'Marriage is no guarantee of fidelity, Eileen.' Look how he had suspected Moira.

'No. Well, you can take my word for it, there was no one else, not on either side. Besides, Carrie's not the sort. To be honest, it isn't so much that she hasn't got it in her to be deceitful, no one's immune from that, she just wasn't serious enough. By that I mean she would not have been happy sneaking about, having secrets and being careful what she said or did. Having an affair is an awful strain, she wouldn't have coped with it.'

Ian wondered if she was speaking from experience. There was a wedding ring on her left hand but Eileen Franks had probably had her fair share of men buzzing around too.

She placed her empty mug on the table as more tears rose and ran down her face. This time they were not so easily stemmed. Ian patted her awkwardly on the shoulder and decided to leave.

He was near enough to the town centre to walk back. His stomach was rumbling, he had had nothing but a slice of toast over seven hours ago. The canteen was the next stop because he could not function when he was hungry.

First he would get someone to find out what they could about Damien Marsh. That idea went out of his mind when he emerged in the reception area through the revolving doors. The place had all the appearance of a late Saturday night. Two uniformed officers were restraining a man who appeared to be drunk, others were standing by in case assistance was required. The cameo performance was entertaining several people who sat on chairs lined against the wall, waiting to make their complaints or report their cat missing or whatever other business had brought them there.

Ian stepped around the skirmish, not wishing to add to the confusion. He stopped at the desk where Sergeant Whitelaw was surveying the scene but without his usual expression of sceptical amusement.

'D and D?'

'No, sir, that's Brian Griffiths.'

'In that case,' he said quietly and faced the mêlée, 'let him go.' Eileen Franks' tears had been difficult to cope with – Ian hated grief in any form because he was helpless to assuage it.

It became quieter, no one moved. Brian Griffiths, although in a group of people, was isolated. His arms now hung loosely at his sides and his face was red from crying. All the fight had gone out of him. The officers stepped out of the way to allow the Chief through. 'It's all right,' he said, 'it'll be all right. Come on, we'll have a talk.'

It was not Ian who had defused the situation; the rage and violence Griffiths had been experiencing had burned themselves out. It was the residue which frightened Ian more, what was left when the truth of the matter really sank in and the whole future had to be faced alone.

To the amazement of everyone present he took Griffiths by the arm and led him from the building in the direction of the nearest pub a hundred yards away.

Brian Griffiths was of mediun height and thin. He looked undernourished, especially now, with one or two old acne scars livid against his face which had paled. Ian virtually pushed him into a seat in the corner and went to the bar. Griffiths, he saw, had no strength left to disappear – nor had he killed his wife, he was certain of that.

'Here, it's a brandy.' It was only a single, it wouldn't do much harm.

Eventually Brian started talking. It had been an ordinary day, he had gone to work leaving Carrie at home because she didn't start until later on Wednesdays. He did not know how the police had found him. 'We were doing Saxborough Road,' he said, 'when this police car pulls up. I thought they were going to one of the houses. I went berserk. I thought they were winding me up. I wanted to go home, to see Carrie, but they wouldn't let me. I tried to get away, then they brought me down here.' He seemed to notice his surroundings for the first time. 'Well, not here. Are they going to arrest me?'

It took Ian a second or two to realise what he meant – not because of Carrie's murder, but because he had put up a struggle.

'No. They were acting for your own protection.' In those

early minutes he might have been capable of anything. And if the officers involved tried to make something of it he would squash it immediately.

'If I find who did it I'll kill him. That's not some idle threat, you know – I mean it.'

Ian believed he did.

'Can I see her now?'

'Not just yet, but today, I promise.' He would have to, to make the official identification. John Cotton might have finished by now; if so, there would be a message waiting for him. 'We'll go back now, Brian, I need to ask you a few things. Don't worry, it won't be too difficult.'

'What the hell do you think you were doing?' Superintendent Thorne was gaping at him in astonishment. 'Just pray the ACC doesn't get to hear of it.'

'It won't happen again, sir.'

'Oh, drop the sir, Mike's normally good enough. I'm telling you for your own good. Just think of your position if he turns out to be our man, and you, a chief inspector, popped down to the local alone with him, to buy him a pint.' He held up a hand to forestall whatever Ian was about to say. 'I accept he probably isn't our man and I trust your judgement, but don't ever let it happen again. Go on, I'm sure you've lots to do.'

Suitably chastened, Ian went back to the control room, his hunger forgotten. It was some time since he had received what he called a good bollocking and, although he avoided dishing them out himself unless it was essential, it had not done him any harm to be reminded of how it felt.

He went over what Brian Griffiths had said, or not said. There had been no unusual circumstances leading up to his wife's death and he claimed it was not necessary for tradesmen to call because he was capable of doing most minor repairs himself. The bigger jobs were the responsibility of the council but nothing had needed attention in their flat since they had lived there. What he said coincided with Eileen

Franks' view of their marriage: there were no stones here to be unturned.

'Extra walkies tonight,' Jim Thomas said grimly to Billy, the border collie who had been both his and Marian's companion and was now his alone. He realised how much his wife had changed over the past year and how much he missed her. No one else had attracted him and he believed the same applied to Marian. Her promotion reflected her recent confidence, but her previous submissiveness was strange because she had seemed relatively assertive before they were married. His one fear was that she would revert if they got back together again. She rarely rang him, which was why he knew it was important this time. She hadn't said much, just that she would appreciate it if he could come over. The tone of her voice told him something was badly wrong.

Billy jumped up as he pulled on a waterproof jacket, eager to be going out again. The rain was hammering down but it was not too far to walk and the firm's car he had access to was in for a service. Fastening Billy's lead he was rewarded by a rough tongue licking his face. In less than fifteen minutes he was knocking on the door of what used to be his home.

'Jim?'

'Yes, it's me.' He refused to use the key she insisted he kept; he did not wish to walk in if she was entertaining or in the bath. 'Jesus! What happened?' he asked as soon as she opened the door. Trying to prevent Billy jumping up at her with one hand he guided her into the lounge with the other. Only when Billy settled down and lay in front of the fire did he sit beside her, an arm around her, and let her cry.

When the sobs had ceased Jim fumbled about in the sideboard and found some vodka. 'I've opened some wine,' Marian told him.

'I'll get you some more. Have you any mixers?' He only drank at weekends but this was an exception. He was shaken by the sight of his wife's bruised face. When he returned with

99

the two glasses Billy was at Marian's feet gazing at her in puzzlement. 'I was seeing this man. Nothing serious. I didn't sleep with him, Jim, I want you to know that. And it sounds so feeble now but I don't even know his proper name. We had a few drinks together and one evening he bought me a meal in the pizza place, but that was as far as it went. I realised he gave me the creeps and I said I didn't want to see him any more.'

'And he did that to you?'

She nodded, wincing as she did so.

'What does this man call himself?' Jim was relieved that the relationship had not progressed beyond a few casual dates but he would find whoever it was and repay him in kind.

'He said everyone calls him Smithy and that I was to call him that as well.'

'What's his address, or phone number?'

Marian shook her head, belatedly seeing the danger in not finding out these things first. 'I don't know.'

Jim refrained from admonishing her. 'The police, have you contacted them yet?' His temper having cooled, he realised it was better to let them deal with the matter – he would only end up with an assault charge himself and make things worse.

'No. But what can they do? I'd prefer to forget it, Jim, he scares me, he might come back if he thinks I'm out to make trouble.'

'Listen, love, there are other people to consider. If he's done it once, he's capable of doing it again and next time someone might not get off so lightly. And this way it will at least be on record.' He did not add, in case he does come back; Marian was scared enough already. Inwardly he was still seething. There wasn't much of his wife, at five feet three and weighing eight stone she was no match for a violent man. He kissed the top of her curly brown head and went to look up the number for the local police station.

They waited. Billy, tongue lolling, looked from one to the other as if he understood the situation and then, seeming to

100

think it would be all right, he stretched out and rested his chin on his paws.

It was almost an hour before the police arrived. The PC who was taking notes kept any surprise under control when Mrs Marian Thomas reported an alleged attack by her boyfriend in front of her husband but he did sigh when she was unable to supply an address.

'I think his first name is Bob. Yes, I'm sure it is. He's a mechanic, if that's any help.'

'And you wish to press charges, madam, *if* we find him?' Robert Smith; it had to be an alias.

'Yes, she does.' It was Jim who replied.

'I just don't want him to come near me again.'

'We'll see what we can do.' PC Freeman left then, with little hope of finding Smith.

'I'm staying the night,' Jim said once they were alone. 'I can sleep down here on the settee, or in the spare room if the bed's made up.'

Marian studied his worried face, not a particularly hand-some face, but dear to her. She would be glad to know he was in the house but she would not ask him to share her bed. Not yet. Apart from which she ached from head to foot. There would be no more grovelling, no more playing the part of the little wife. Marian Thomas felt she was beginning to grow up.

Robert Smith was not an alias. 'Someone has to be called it, I suppose,' the night patrol sergeant commented. 'Go and see him, two of you. It's only eleven thirty, he might still be up.' With three murders on their doorstep they could not afford to take chances. It probably wasn't their man, he'd hit the woman, not tried to strangle her, and it was a quiet night, the men could be spared.

PC Freeman and PC Platt headed towards the house of Robert Smith not even sure if it was the right Smith, but Mrs Thomas had said he lived in Rickenham Green and always met her on foot so it had to be assumed his address was fairly central. The other R. Smiths were not.

Smithy smiled at the two men on his doorstep. She didn't waste much time, he thought, as he asked them to come in.

The small house was immaculately neat, the daily paper folded on a polished coffee table, no crumbs or threads on the carpet. PC Freeman took a surreptitious look at Smith's hands but there was no redness about the knuckles and no obvious marks elsewhere. If he had hit Mrs Thomas, it was with an open palm. He was not a small man; he could have inflicted far more damage had he chosen.

Robert Smith confirmed he had been seeing Marian. 'We went out a few times, I thought we were getting on all right. I really did. We had some laughs and she was nice. I knew she was married, but separated, you understand I thought we might make a go of it. Women. Shows how wrong you can be.'

'And you were at her house tonight?'

'I was.' He shook his head. 'She invited me over for a meal but as soon as I got there she said she didn't want to see me again. Look, I know why you're here.' Smith bowed his head. 'I hit her, I admit it. We argued and it all got a bit nasty. She said some things ... well, that's best forgotten. I hit her and she fell over, I didn't mean to hurt her, that's not my style. I apologised and left. I can understand she's frightened but you can reassure her I won't go near her again. I give you my word.' He sat in the Dralon-covered armchair, a defeated man. 'God, I've never done anything like that in my life. I was hurt, I suppose, it's no excuse. Tell her I'm sorry, will you, please?'

PC Freeman nodded. 'Mr Smith, where do you work?'

'I don't.'

'I'm sorry, I understood that – '

'None of this puts me in a good light, does it? I told Marian I was a mechanic. Was is the operative word. I used to be. I can't get a job at the moment, I'm unemployed. You can check. I was just trying to impress her.'

'Do you own any form of transport?'

'No.' Smith's tone was puzzled. 'Why?'

'We'll need you to make a statement, Mr Smith, but under the circumstances it can wait until the morning. Mrs Thomas may change her mind about pressing charges. If she doesn't, someone will be expecting you about nine.'

'How will I know?'

'You can telephone. You have a phone?'

'Yes. It's in the kitchen.'

PC Freeman made a note of the number. 'Good-night.'

Robert Smith showed them to the door and closed it after them, smiling ruefully. He had been wrong about Marian, he had not thought she was the sort to go to the police. However, he would comply with their wishes and be there at nine if she did not change her mind. Why those questions, he wondered as he made a cup of tea, inmdiately wiping a few spilled spots off the work surface. They could check with the DVLA, he didn't have a car, and he was, after all, unemployed.

PCs Freeman and Platt reported in accordingly, leaving Smith's details on file. The whole thing had the look of the usual scene of domestic violence – a row, escalating into verbal, then physical violence – but the sergeant was right, no stone could be left unturned. No doubt CID would follow up if they thought it necessary, but the computer already showed he had no previous record. They set off once more after a complaint from a resident that music was still coming from a back-street pub and that he thought there was some after-hours drinking going on. This public-spirited man refused to give his name – probably, they guessed, because he was known to the landlord.

'Damn it.' Ian had forgotten his intention of finding out a bit more about Damien Marsh. 'I want it done discreetly,' he instructed when he allocated the job. 'If his parents find out they'll have a bunch of briefs making our lives a misery. Try

the school first, see if you can find out who his friends are.'
He did not say that the headmaster was just going to love
another reappearance, they would find that out for
themselves.

It had been a long day. Brian Griffiths had finally made the
official identification of the body and seemed to take comfort
in the fact that she had been neither mutilated nor sexually
abused. It was all he had to hold on to.

'You look shattered,' Moira told him as he kissed the top of
her head, an easy enough feat as she only reached his
shoulder.

'I am. I'm going to have a bath.'

Moira had heard the outlines on the news. All Carrie's
relatives lived in Rickenham and had been informed before it
was broadcast. She dared not think what would happen if
they did not find the killer soon. As it was, there were media
people all over the town, hanging around outside the police
station but being kept at a discreet distance from the victims'
houses. It would not be long before they found out where the
three husbands were staying. She pitied them, they were not
to be allowed to grieve in peace. But she understood it was a
big story and would have to be covered. 'I'll run the water for
you,' she volunteered. She rarely ran around after him but he
did look awful and she knew it would help him relax. He was
a pain when he was tense.

When he came down in a loudly striped robe which Mark
had bought him for Christmas and which showed his strong
legs to good advantage, Moira was nursing a glass of wine
and flicking through a magazine. It was too late to bother with
a proper meal so she heated a tin of soup and made omelettes.

'The Chief Constable has made his views clear, and I can't
blame him. We're not exactly blazing a trail of glory.'

'You know what he's like, Ian, it's only because he hates
appearing on television.' It was true, and he would have to
spend the evening preparing a carefully worded, bland statement for the press and the national news. 'I know it isn't easy
for you, but think of those women's families.'

Slumped in a chair, Ian looked defeated. 'I really don't get it. The relatives' alibis are watertight. But there's something about the three of them that we're not seeing.'

'I'm going up. Shall I set the alarm?'

'Yes, please, love.'

'Don't be long.'

Ian seemed not to hear her. He eyed the whisky bottle and decided one would do no harm. Tomorrow they might have more on Damien Marsh but he would also find out exactly where Jason Proctor and Alastair Harvey had been at the relevant time, for both had a connection with at least one of the women.

Dawn was still half an hour away when he grabbed the clock and fumbled for the knob to kill its insistent ringing. Although he hated the noise it was more effective than the clock radio they used to have. He cursed as he stood on his slippers. Today it was going to start all over again: another round of questioning; more correlation of facts; more forensic evidence. But would it get them anywhere?

Washed and shaved he felt more human and the smell of bacon sizzling under the grill told him how hungry he was. He had eaten little the previous day. Bacon was an unusual treat on a weekday now that Mark had gone. Had Mark heard about these murders? Surely he must have done. He had not rung though, which hurt Ian. He hoped the boy wasn't drifting away from them, but was honest enough to admit that he had not spent as much time with his son as he might have done.

Street lights from the road behind showed up the undulating branches of the bare trees at the bottom of the garden as the wind bent them to its will. The patio paving stones were dry once more and some dead leaves skittered noisily across them. Ian ate a bacon sandwich standing up and left Moira, still in her dressing-gown, to make her own way to work.

From the lounge window she watched him drive away, as drawn as yesterday, but now he also looked ill. She would not tell him so because he would start to think he was. She sighed. It was the life he had chosen, one he loved, and although she

105

did not fully understand his crusade against crime she admired him for his determination, his belief that if you strived hard enough, anything was possible. It was, for a pessimistic man, a rather optimistic theory. A self-mocking smile was reflected in the bathroom mirror when she went upstairs to shower. Who was she to criticise? Her ambitions had once been no higher than to be a good wife and mother, and with a college education at that. Now Mark had grown up and she had her job, but she wanted more – the two men no longer filled her life. Deciding exactly what it was she wanted was the difficult part, further education maybe, or a better job. There was no rush, it would come to her in time. For the moment she concentrated on getting ready to form some semblance of order in the chaos that was John Freeling's office.

Barry Swan's sporty car followed Ian's into the car-park. They walked across to the station together, heads down against the wind, both early because the post-mortem was early. Other, less urgent cases – accidents and a hospital death – had been rescheduled because three consecutive murders took priority. All they had time for was a quick glance at some telephone messages and another result from Huntingdon before they were off again.

The pathologist on duty at the hospital mortuary was Julian Ling. He was impatient to start, he had a busy day ahead of him. No introductions were necessary as they all knew each other. Once more Doc Harris was thwarted as his morning surgery was already in progress. 'We'll begin then, Ian, if you're ready?' Julian Ling bent his head to his work so his smile could not be seen. Poor old Ian, after all these years he still could not stomach it. He worked quickly and methodically, speaking into the microphone above his head as he went. It saved so much time later, a secretary simply typed it up straight from the cassette.

'It's much of a muchness,' Julian said as he stripped off his rubber gloves, leaving his assistant to tidy the body up. 'Healthy young woman, no injuries other than the marks on her neck, except in this case the nail parings are more interesting. Not sure what it is until after the analysis.'

'Did she struggle?'

'No signs of it – you saw yourself there was no bruising, other than in the neck area – but it's possible she might have grabbed at something, some part of his clothing. Did you manage to avoid the newshounds? They've been out there since the crack of dawn.'

'More or less.' They had simply walked straight past the several men and women who were waiting with cameras and notebooks but who would not be expecting any comment until after it was over. Ian was recognisable because of his television appearance. 'It's getting out that bothers me.'

'There's always the fire escape.'

'We're on the ground floor, Julian.'

'I think he means we go upstairs then out the back way,' Barry said. He had his own way of coping, he kept his eyes focused six inches above the level of the corpse; after all, he could still hear what Julian was saying. 'It's worth a try.' It was the coward's way of going about it. They were not obliged to say anything to the press, the usual 'no comment at this stage' kind of remark would have sufficed, but if the reporters were hanging around here thinking the police were still inside they would be off someone else's back.

'No time for a snifter today, chaps.' He indicated a trolley being wheeled in. 'I've got another customer waiting.'

Surprisingly there was no one at the bottom of the fire escape and they managed to get to the car before they were spotted. They pulled out into the road, each with a grim smile of satisfaction.

John Cotton and his team had been as thorough as always. He confirmed that there were cat hairs everywhere and that anyone who had entered that flat would be unlikely to have escaped without taking one or two with them. Ian had noticed a white one clinging to the side of his own shoe after he had

107

left. It was no more than a pin-point of hope. This man was clever, always remaining one step ahead of them. It was possible he went to the lengths of destroying all that he wore each time. And it's still possible it's more than one person, Ian reminded himself.

The personal effects belonging to Carrie Griffiths which related to her financial affairs and social engagements, including her diary, were spread out on a trestle table. Ian was about to take a look for himself when DS Markham said he had important news concerning Damien Marsh. 'In here,' Ian said, opening the door to an unoccupied side room.

'He knew all three.' Ian held his breath. 'Roy Orchard taught him, but he knew Debbie through the school as he told you. Not only did he live in the house next to Mrs Baxter, her husband said she gave him a lift once, but he doesn't know where or why. And this is the best bit. Damien used to go around with Carrie Griffiths' brother, Simon Johns, and both of them have been pulled in suspected of shop-lifting and one or two other minor offences. No charges brought against them though.'

'How do we know this?'

'DC Campbell and DC Gibbons spent most of yesterday with the Johns family. I telephoned to ask them to throw the name into the conversation if possible, see if it got a reaction.'

'Why wasn't I told this last night?'

'Because we didn't know until this morning. The family were upset, too upset to be coherent. DC Gibbons went back this morning and tried again.'

'Good for her.' Brenda Gibbons had recently joined them but Ian was not sure yet whether she was a natural detective or whether she was being over-conscientious until she got her feet under the table. 'Has he been brought in?'

'No. Your instructions were to tread carefully. Now?' Markham asked, standing up.

'Yes. Now.'

Ian remained in the side room. It would explain everything, except the motive. Virginia Baxter knew Damien as a neighbour and had once given him a lift; obviously she would let him in if he knocked at the door. He was staying with friends at the time but no one had yet been able to determine who they were or where they lived, and he had his own car. Roy had taught him; it was not beyond the bounds of possibility that Damien knew where he lived, perhaps he had had reason to go to the house at some time. And he had known Carrie's brother; had knocked around with him several years ago – Carrie would still have been living at home then but it would not be difficult to find her new address. Then why did he think they were wrong? Damien Marsh was a petulant, spoilt youth who struck him as not having the intelligence or the energy to commit the crimes – if things did not fall into his lap; he would put them out of his mind. Unless, of course, the motive was a drug habit. It was true that nothing had been stolen and that blackmail seemed unlikely: bank statements and building society accounts for all parties showed no unusual or unexpected withdrawals and the Griffithses would not have had the wherewithal to make such payments.

It would be interesting to hear what young Damien had to say for himself, but before Markham returned with him Ian received a telephone call.

'I suppose it has to be true sometimes,' he told Barry when it transpired that Marsh's partner was indeed a friend of the Chief Constable.

'What did he say? The CC?'

'Only that he didn't want any complaints and that Marsh was an awkward customer, it was just a reminder to do things by the book. Do you want to speak to the lad?'

'But surely you – '

Ian held up a hand. 'No. I've got preconceived ideas. You haven't met him.'

The expression of surprise on Barry's face remained there for several seconds after Ian had gone.

Carrie Griffiths' financial state was no match for the Baxters' or even near that of the Orchards. There was a cheque-book, in joint names, the stub of which showed a credit balance of forty-six pounds which, Ian calculated, was some pounds below what it actually was as Carrie rounded her transactions up to the nearest pound whenever she wrote a cheque. There was also a joint building society passbook in which regular weekly deposits were recorded. The amounts varied between five and fifteen pounds and represented the savings required to escape from Magnolia House to which Eileen Franks had referred. They had amassed almost five hundred pounds during the eleven months of their marriage. To the Griffiths it was a large sum, to a blackmailer it would be peanuts. Ian picked up the diary and studied the address and telephone section. Alan Campbell would have already correlated the names, but nowhere in any of the cases did the name of Damien Marsh appear, nor did his home telephone number. He flicked through the appointments pages, which yielded very little. Either Carrie had no appointments or she did not bother to note them down. A couple of pages had been used as shopping lists. On the top right-hand corner of a date late in January was a cross, and another, four weeks later, for the day before she died. He knew what they signified, Moira did the same – they were nothing more sinister than the dates of her menstrual cycle which was confirmed by the post-mortem. He was about to replace the diary when he froze. Had no one else noticed? On the front was the name of one of the big bookmakers. Gambling? His mind raced. How much violence had been committed over the years in the name of betting? Not that for one moment he suspected Ladbroke's of sending the boys round, but gambling sometimes led to debts, to money being borrowed, and money lenders were not renowned for altruism or generosity. He could not recall seeing any statistics on the subject, but surely women preferred roulette or bingo. Carrie Griffiths went to bingo. Had these three women become addicted, hidden the fact from their husbands and borrowed money which they had finally been unable to repay? No. It didn't scan. What use was a dead debtor? But the Ladbroke's diary was Carrie's possession, not her husband's.

On the way up to his office Ian asked a passing officer to

arrange for some coffee to be sent up. He registered the vague annoyance his request produced and raised his eyebrows wryly. He rarely pulled rank but occasionally he had to prove himself still capable of it.

On his desk lay the diary. Ian stared at it. The only time he had a bet was on one of the big races, the National or the Derby, or on the correct score of a football match when Norwich were playing. He had found that, despite his obsession with the game, and his knowledge of it, it was not exactly a profitable business. When his coffee arrived he picked up the telephone and asked the operator to put him through to the nearest branch of Ladbroke's. If she was surprised at the request it did not come across in her voice.

'I'll try, sir. Oh, is it that time already? In that case there will be somebody there.'

'Why shouldn't there be?'

'Most betting shops don't open until at least ten fifteen or ten thirty.'

How interesting. Perhaps all females were knowledgeable about the racing world. 'Tell me,' he said, 'do you know much about it?'

'Not really. It's just that my uncle's the manager of a shop.'

'In that case you might be able to save me a call. They don't open early . . .'

'No, sir, but there's often someone in to settle the previous day's bets, that's if they haven't done so the night before.'

'OK. Pardon my ignorance, but how would you go about getting a Ladbroke's diary? Would you need to be an account customer, for instance?'

'Oh, that's easy, you just go into one of their shops and get one. What they usually do is sell them for a pound, which is cheap enough anyway, but there's a one-pound voucher for a free bet inside. So if you use it, the diary's free.'

'Good marketing idea. It means you have to go back.'

'I shouldn't think they've got any left now.'

Ian was amused to think that the faceless individual he was conversing with imagined his only interest was in a free diary. 'Do you have a bet yourself?' This informal little chat was illuminating, or so he thought. There was a pause.

'No, I do not.' The 'sir' was deliberately delayed.

He had overstepped the mark. 'Ah, good, fine,' he said before replacing the receiver. The battered Yellow Pages in the drawer told him there was a branch of Ladbroke's not far from Magnolia House. Barry would be ensconced with Damien Marsh, so he would take himself down there. 'Do we know where Harvey and Proctor were on Wednesday morning?' he inquired of DC Campbell before he left.

'Harvey says he was out at an auction – we're still checking on that – but Proctor's out of it. Damaged his hand while he was working on a car the day before. He's in plaster. The hospital confirmed he's broken two fingers.' Campbell handed him a file. 'House-to-house.'

Door-knocking in the Magnolia House area was a fruitless exercise; too many people had too much to hide and those who might have seen anything would not put themselves out to tell the police. Nevertheless they pressed on. Ian glanced at the file and placed it on the desk.

The betting shop was doing a tidy trade. There were a handful of customers who had nothing else to do and nowhere to go and used it as a social centre, which, to Ian's surprise, it did rather resemble. There were comfortable chairs and plenty of tables, a surfeit of racing newspapers and banks of television screens on which could be seen sporting events both current and past and the starting prices of all the races. There were even personal screens at some of the tables where the punter could conjure up whatever it was he was interested in. A vending machine stood in the corner and there was a container of iced water. It was a far cry from the squalid back-street premises which had existed in the fifties before off-course betting had become legalised. And there were ashtrays everywhere. No fashionable health obsessions, here. Ian took advantage of it and lit up.

The young man behind the counter placed several betting slips through the computerised, timed machine before Ian was able to speak to him. He produced a photograph of Carrie Griffiths but met with a blank.

'We get to know most of the regulars, but I've never seen her before. I'll ask Mr Jackson if he knows her.' Mr Jackson did not but came out from the office behind when he heard the police were on the premises.

'I can't help you, I'm afraid.' Carrie Griffiths' photograph had not yet been released to the press but he remembered the name. 'It's her, isn't it? The poor girl who was murdered? Wait a minute, doesn't her husband come in on a Saturday?' He was speaking to the other man.

'A bloke called Brian Griffiths, yeah, but I don't know if it's her husband.'

'Does he bet heavily?' Ian asked.

'No. Same bet every week, a ten-pence each way Yankee, costs him two pounds forty-two because he always pays the tax. He picks outsiders – if they ever come up he'll be on to a fortune.'

Ian was saddened by this revelation. Brian Griffiths had probably put on his couple of quid each week just as others did the Lottery, hoping to come up so he could provide a better home for Carrie. And his theory had been shattered too – gambling seemed to be ruled out. Brian had purchased the diary and must have given it to his wife.

DC Brenda Gibbons was at Magnolia House at that moment speaking to the residents they had not been able to see the previous day. One of the flats on the second floor housed a family of four who were on the waiting list for somewhere bigger. 'We keep ourselves to ourselves round here,' the father said from his sprawled position on the sofa.

'We don't know anything,' his wife added, picking up one of the fretful children. 'She gave me a hand up with the pushchair once, when the lift wasn't working, never spoke to her otherwise. She was a hairdresser, wasn't she? I kept meaning to ask her to do my hair, being a neighbour, like, I'm

113

sure she'd have done it cheap. Too late now.' DC Gibbons noted there was no sorrow, no pity, only regret for a missed opportunity. The people round here were a hard lot.

There was a better response from the flat next door to Carrie's. It was opened a few inches and a wizened face peered out, breaking into a smile when Brenda Gibbons explained who she was. 'Come in, come in.' This was unexpected behaviour for Magnolia House.

'I was over at my brother's place yesterday. I always stay the night because it's such a long journey by bus and I don't like coming home in the dark. What was it you wanted?' Mrs Bennett, hardly a prime suspect, had been asked about her movements the previous day. She was genuinely distressed when she heard of Carrie's death. 'That poor child, that poor little child. This place is getting worse every day.' She sat heavily in a chair, her hands shaking as she clasped them in her lap. 'She did my hair once, you know, and she wouldn't take a penny. I bought her a packet of cigarettes, though, I knew she smoked. And her husband, a nice enough young man in his way.' She clutched at the neck of her Viyella blouse as if it was a form of protection. A look of anguish passed over her face but she did not cry. Mrs Bennett had had a life of disappointment and pain, there were no tears left.

'Can I get you something?' Brenda Gibbons sank on to her haunches.

'No, dear, I'll be all right in a minute. Unless you'd like a cup of tea?' At this idea she perked up. 'Just a quick cup?'

'I'd love one, but I really can't stay. Thanks all the same.'

'I've got a lot of time for you people,' she said as she politely went to open the door, 'and I don't envy you your jobs one bit. When the flats got broken into a couple of years back a really pleasant young man came to see me. Now, I watch enough television to know no one hardly ever gets their things back, but do you know what? I did. Nothing valuable, just a few bits of jewellery from my husband and son. I can't wear the rings now, you see.' She held out her gnarled, arthritic hands. 'But I'll never forget that young fellow and he even

114

took the trouble of returning them to me himself. Markham, his name was. When you see him tell him Mrs Bennett sends her regards.'

Brenda Gibbons bit her lip and lowered her eyes. 'I'll do that,' she said. 'Now, don't forget to put your chain on.'

'Markham! She's got to be joking, hasn't she?' DC Emmanuel couldn't believe it when Brenda related the story. 'That's the first time I've heard him described as pleasant. There must be a side to him we don't know.'

It was Winston who interviewed the lorry driver in the flat opposite. He was not too happy about being woken up although it was after eleven and it was clear he had had a heavy night. He was unshaven and wearing a vest and track suit bottoms in which he had slept. Empty cans littered the floor alongside some fish and chip paper. The air was fetid with beer and sweat. He had not lived there long and had only seen Carrie once: he was on the road a lot of the time, mainly on the Continent so he was away overnight. With a mug of instant coffee in his hand he was more awake and willingly supplied the name of the firm for whom he worked, explaining everything was logged so it would not be difficult to find out exactly where he was at the time. He might be a slob, Winston thought as he left the building and went to join DC Gibbons, but I think he's an honest slob.

Mrs Bennett's comments were passed on to Markham, who merely grunted, but word soon got around. For several days, whenever his presence was required someone would say, 'Anyone know where that pleasant young man is?'

7

Tom Marsh had tried to insist that he sit in on the interview with his son. Fortunately for DS Swan, Damien was no longer a juvenile and therefore a parent or guardian was not required.

'Yeah,' he said in response to Barry's initial question as to whether he understood why he was there and how the interview was to be conducted. His next three answers took the same form and Barry wondered if Damien was mentally handicapped in some way, which would necessitate the presence of Marsh senior.

'The day that Mrs Baxter was murdered, where were you, Damien?'

'Staying with friends.'

Barry was relieved. The boy could speak. He smiled reassuringly. 'Locally? Damien, I said locally?'

Damien looked up. He was of medium height and build but had the appearance of unfitness for someone his age. His almost black hair was lank and although his mouth retained its sullen mould there was a hint of fear in his eyes. 'Look, will my parents need to know about what's said in here?'

'Not if you don't want them to.' Or unless you're guilty and it comes out in court, he added silently. 'What is it you want to tell me?'

'I wasn't where my parents thought I was, I was here, in Rickenham.'

'I need to know exactly where, Damien.'

'I can't tell you.' His head dropped again.

'Look, you're almost nineteen, why is it so important your

mother and father don't know where you were? You're of age, you can please yourself.'

'I can't.'

'Damien, I want to remind you again why you are here. We are investigating three murders and you are the only person we can find so far who knew all the victims. Do you understand your position?' It was not the sort of information he should be giving out but he needed to get at the truth.

'And you think I killed them.'

'We just want to know where you were at the relevant times. Now, let's start with Mrs Baxter again. You were in Rickenham Green. Where and with whom?'

'Paula,' he said quickly. 'I was with Paula.'

'Does she have a surname?'

Damien bit his lip. 'Bishop.'

'Paula Bishop. Fine. Now . . .' Barry stopped. Paula Bishop? Surely he didn't mean the wife of David Bishop, one of the doctors at Rickenham General? Bishop was a common enough name but Paula wasn't. Damien was watching him with a defiant smile. 'All right, you were with Paula Bishop. Where did you go?'

'To her house.' And then, realising it had to come out if he was to prove his innocence, he gave the address. 'She's a friend of my mother's, I met her at one of the parties my parents are forever having.' As he talked he became more animated and Barry began to understand that the boy was half-way in love with Paula Bishop, a woman almost twice his age, and that the reason for his demeanour was partly disappointed love. Paula Bishop was not about to leave her husband for Damien and he was not experienced enough to realise that the episode would be no more than a pleasant memory in a few years' time. He hoped, for David Bishop's sake, that he was on duty when his wife was interviewed. David had been away on a course when Damien stayed the night with her; the rest of the time he was genuinely with the friends where the Marshes believed him to be.

For the next hour and a half they went over his relationships

117

with Debbie Orchard and Carrie Griffiths. 'Carrie was all right, but she was mostly out with Brian if I went round there to see Simon.'

'You and Simon, you were caught shoplifting, I believe.'

'We were younger then, still at school. The store called my parents and they said if I mixed with any of the Johnses again they'd stop my allowance.'

'And did you?'

'No, I never went back there after that.'

'And now?'

'Now?'

'I understand you aren't employed – do you still get an allowance?'

'Yes, but if they find out about . . . well, what I told you . . .' He did not need to finish the sentence. Damien Marsh, brought up to have everything without effort, would not find a place in the real world easy to cope with.

Barry interrupted the interview, turning off the recording machine and, on the pretext of organising a cup of coffee, made arrangements for someone to go and see Paula Bishop.

Damien could not recall where he was on the date of Debbie's death but thought he was at home with his mother when Carrie was killed. DS Swan glanced at the detective who was sitting in with him to see if there were any questions he wanted to add but they had been through it all more than once. Damien denied having any sort of relationship with the two other women; he had an alibi for one of the murders, possibly two, and the reason Mrs Baxter had given him a lift was because his car was in the garage having a wing straightened out after he'd been involved in an accident. 'There's no bus stop for a hell of a way. Mrs Baxter knew that and stopped when she saw me walking. Of course, if either of my parents were in, I could've borrowed one of their cars or they'd've run me into town.'

After five hours they let him go.

*

Jim Thomas left Marian's house in time for work the following morning but only after she reassured him that she felt fine and was going in herself. 'I'll make some excuse. No one knows I was seeing anyone, I'll say I walked into the kitchen cupboard or something.' It was believable, all the bruising was to one side. The last thing she wanted was to be alone in the house in case Smithy returned.

Neither Jim nor Marian noticed how easily they sat together in the kitchen over tea and toast, just as when they were living together. Jim kept his eyes averted from her face because, in a strange way, he felt partly responsible for her injuries. If he had tried harder to make her understand that he preferred her how she had been prior to their marriage to how she had become, they might still be together and she would not have met Smith.

It was half-way through the morning that Marian came to the conclusion that she did not want to see Smithy again under any circumstances and she certainly did not want the whole thing dragged up in several months' time when it came to court. During a quiet period she went out into the street and used a public telephone kiosk to inform the police that she wished to drop the charge and would call in on her way home to sign a form to that effect. It was with a sense of relief that she replaced the receiver and went back to work.

Robert Smith made two telephone calls before leaving the house the following morning. The second confirmed that his presence was required at the station. He walked the relatively short distance to make his statement.

Ian had already been made aware of the events of the previous night. By the time Smith had signed his statement he was also aware that the man was, as he had said, unemployed and was not in possession of a motor vehicle or a criminal record. Nevertheless, he directed the interviewing officer to casually ask where he was on the dates of the murders. Smith had been unable to remember, but why should he? Unemployed, he probably found one day much like another and he seemed completely baffled by the line of questioning. And would he, Ian wondered, have turned up if he had anything to hide? He had had all night to make a run for it.

There was further disappointment when the results showed that the interesting fingernail scrapings Julian Ling had pointed out were no more than the result of the chemicals Carrie Griffiths used as part of her job.

When Robert Smith walked out through the revolving doors he wondered how long it would be before he was sentenced and what he would get. There would be no need for a trial as he had already admitted his guilt. He thought about it. First offence: a suspended sentence and a slap on the wrist seemed to be appropriate, but he felt sick at the idea of possessing any sort of criminal record.

It was not until several days later when he received the communication from the police through the post that he knew that Marian Thomas had decided, after all, to drop the charges. He laughed with relief at his own foolishness. He ought to have guessed she would do so.

Alastair Harvey was finding difficulties in proving he really was at that auction. He had gone off in the van at eight fifteen and driven the sixty-odd miles to the country house where the contents were being sold. Unfortunately no other dealers he knew were present and he saw why once he had inspected the lots. All the good stuff must have been siphoned off somewhere by the bankrupt family, what remained were pieces of ugly Victorian furniture and things his expertise told him would be difficult to resell. The other dealers must have come on the preview date when neither he nor Charles had been available. A lot of the customers, he guessed, were private individuals looking for single items for their own homes. They had been welcome to it.

If the police wanted to make a thing of it, all they had to do was contact the auctioneers, see who else was there and find someone who remembered seeing him. There were not many men with the reddish-blond hair of Alastair Harvey; he would even supply a photograph.

'I really don't know, Ian. A lot'll depend on what Paula Bishop has to say. Damien's into older women – well one at least – and like the others, she hasn't got any kids. If she denies he was with her we're back to square one.' Mrs Marsh had already said Damien was not with her on the morning when Carrie was killed because, ironically, but coincidentally, she was at the hairdresser's herself, but a different one. Barry had also followed up the story about the car being repaired. It was true. It had gone to the nearest BMW dealers, as they suspected, not to the likes of Mr Proctor and his son.

'Who's gone to see Paula Bishop?'

'I sent DC Gibbons.'

'Alone?'

'I thought it best, under the circumstances.'

'To protect David, you mean?'

'Yes.' Barry's face reddened slightly and he brushed back his hair with a characteristic gesture of embarrassment. It was his job, his duty, to help solve these murders, if people got hurt in the process it was too bad. If people behaved themselves in these matters no one would be hurt. 'Duty and compassion can be combined if you go about it the right way.'

Ian laughed. 'Don't be so bloody pompous, Swan. Are we waiting for the delectable Brenda Gibbons to return or are you allowed out tonight?'

'God, you do annoy me at times. It's not a case of being allowed out, Lucy . . .'

'I know, I know. Come on, I'll buy.' Ian was still laughing. There were times when he could rattle Barry easily. And Lucy Swan, Lucy Clarke that was, had succeeded where most women fail. She had changed her man.

121

But not that much, Ian realised when, at half-past ten, Barry rang first for a taxi then his wife. They shared the taxi as far as the traffic lights then Ian jumped out. 'There will be trouble ahead,' he sang as a parting shot.

DC Brenda Gibbons was not, as several of her superiors suspected, just getting her feet under the table. She was unaware how good she was. The reason for her success was not so much that she always knew what she was doing – like many other women in the modern service, she looked nothing like a detective and had the sort of face that made people like her and a manner which made them want to confide in her. She mistakenly believed the same applied to all her colleagues.

DS Swan had sent her off before Damien Marsh was released because he did not want to risk him contacting Paula and concocting some story if he had not actually been with her. The affair might be a figment of his imagination but Barry suspected otherwise. Damien would look a complete fool in Mrs Bishop's eyes if it were not true.

Paula Bishop was likeable, she laughed easily, she was quick-witted and she knew how to dress. She left strangers with the impression that she was beautiful, although in fact she was only averagely attractive. She had done what many before her had wished to do, taken up nursing in the hope of marrying a doctor. Her motives for marrying David might have been calculating but she loved him in her own way. Now that she was in a position where she did not need to work, she no longer did so. Paradoxically, David, with private patients on the side, worked longer hours and Paula discovered what boredom was. When she worked in obstetrics there was no spare time to do half the things she would have liked to do; she wondered if the constant contact with babies had put her off having one of her own or if she would have felt that way whatever career she had chosen. It was still not too late, as David repeatedly pointed out.

'Hello,' she said, her surprise evident in her tone.

'Detective Gibbons,' Brenda said, smiling at the fractionally overweight lady with her thick, fair hair plaited in the French style.

'Is something wrong? It's not David, is it?'

'No, nothing like that. May I come in for a minute?'

'Of course. I'm sorry.'

Brenda Gibbons was impressed. The detached Victorian house had been thoroughly modernised and shouted luxury whichever way she turned. She was shown into the spacious lounge. The preamble over, Brenda set about the delicate task of inquiring about Paula's relationship with the Marshes' son.

'I've known Tom and Jean for six or seven years. We met at a mutual acquaintance's house. Jean told me they've stepped up their own security after what happened. Still, if they could get into the Baxters' place, they could get in anywhere.'

'And Damien?' Brenda Gibbons watched carefully for any reaction to the name. There was none.

'They've spoiled him, of course, but it so often happens with only children. He's not so bad. If only he smiled a bit more, he takes life far too seriously for one so young.'

'Has he been here?'

'I can't . . . yes, he came one Christmas with Tom and Jean.'

'Just the once?'

'Yes, I've just said so. Look, am I a suspect or something, because if so I want my solicitor here.'

'Is there any reason for me to think you might be a suspect?' But DC Gibbons had spotted all the obvious signs of guilt. 'Perhaps there's something worrying you.' She leant forward with the natural body language of a good listener. 'The thing is, Mrs Bishop, Damien could be in serious trouble. He has told us a couple of things we need to confirm are true.'

'Oh God.' Paula's poise had deserted her. 'It's up to me, isn't it? If he's charged or whatever, it'll all come out. Yes, he was here. Just a minute.' She went out of the room and returned with her handbag from which she produced a small diary. 'It was when David was away. Here.' She held the open pages so they could both see them. It was the right date. She sat down again. 'God knows what you must think of me.'

'I'm not here to judge, Mrs Bishop.'

'I honestly don't know how it happened, or why I let it. It was just so bloody flattering. No,' she shook her head, 'I shan't make any excuses. I enjoyed it while it lasted. Will this need to be made public?'

'Possibly not, but I can't promise anything.'

'Poor David.'

'I think that's all I need to know, but you will have to come and make a formal statement.'

'Now?'

'Well, yes, if it's convenient.'

'Yes. Now. I want to get it out of the way.' She ran upstairs for a coat because it looked as if it might rain again.

So much for coming home early, Moira thought when she saw the tell-tale flush on her husband's face and smelled his beery breath. At least he had warned her in advance. His meal was in the oven, covered in tinfoil and probably dry but she doubted if he would notice. She had to admit the night out had done him good: the lines of strain were less prominent and when he got into bed he fell immediately into a deep sleep and woke refreshed the following morning.

Superintendent Thorne asked to see him just before twelve. They were all getting twitchy. The few leads they had were dead ends and, not having met Damien Marsh, Thorne thought things still pointed his way. 'When did you last have a day off?' he asked Ian, who could not remember. 'Then take my advice, push off for the afternoon – you can't be involved every step of the way and you won't do yourself or us any good if you go down with something. Now, delivery firms, any connections there?'

'None that we've come up with. Some of them don't keep proper records, we're speaking to individual drivers now.' It would take forever, and there would be the ones who did a spot of driving on the side, jobs that the DHS would like to know about. It wouldn't get them anywhere but, like so much of their work, it had to be done.

Surprising himself, Ian took Mike Thorne's advice. First he stopped at the control room. 'Get them to speak to everyone on that list again. All the delivery firms. This time I want to know who all the drivers are, on the books or otherwise.' He did not wait to see the despair on the officers' faces before shutting the door behind him.

For almost ten minutes he sat in the car listening to the soothing patter of rain on the roof. However much or little happened that afternoon he was not going to be part of it and he was looking forward to a bit of space. But where to go? Moira was at work and he did not fancy sitting glued to the television in an empty house. It was too wet to walk any distance, not that walking was one of his favourite occupations unless Moira was there to chivvy him along. Once, some years ago, he had been lucky enough to come across a notice advertising the mid-week afternoon kick-off of the semi-final of a non-league cup match between Rickenham Athletic and some club he could no longer remember. No such luck today.

'Damn it.' He got out of the car and walked quickly up the High Street towards the Crown. It was time he took up a hobby. What on earth was he going to do with himself when he retired if he couldn't amuse himself for one afternoon now? And unless he could persuade her otherwise, Moira would be working long after he stopped.

Two pints and a ham sandwich later, he felt quite mellow. Unfortunately, or perhaps fortunately, the Crown was not a pub which stayed open all day. He thanked the landlord and wandered back to the main shopping area with the vague idea of buying a proper newspaper and sitting in a quiet pub to read it all. Rarely did he have time for such luxuries. Then for no explicable reason, unless because it was raining harder than ever, he found himself in the brightly lit foyer of the

Savoy Cinema staring at the posters. He bought a ticket and headed for the area allocated to Screen 3.

DS Markham had gone back to speak to the Johns family again. There were a lot of them and they were close knit. And there was the slight chance that here might lie the key to it all. Simon Johns had progressed from shoplifting to theft from houses and had twice been on probation. Next time he would go inside. If Simon had not killed his sister, he did know Damien. And Damien had known all three women. Had someone else been made aware of their existence?

It was not a successful visit. The house was crowded and noisy and Carrie's mother still cried inconsolably. 'She was so young,' she repeated, 'far too young to die.' And then, as he tried to speak to Simon, one of her inconsequential comments registered. 'I hadn't even finished paying for her birthday present,' she said. Markham knew this was not callousness; the bereaved often latch on to trivial things to prevent themselves thinking of the real issue.

'When was her birthday, Mrs Johns?' It was on the file, of course, but suddenly it seemed relevant. If Carrie's birthday was that recent she might have had something delivered.

'A couple of weeks ago.' Mrs Johns then produced some photographs and the cuttings from the *Herald* from the time Carrie had finished her hairdressing apprenticeship. He left after that and returned to the station. DC Gibbons was on her way to the canteen as he crossed the floor of the reception.

'Want to show me just what a pleasant young man you are and buy me a coffee?' she said.

'Give me a few minutes. But you can pay. There's such a thing as equality, you know.' Markham's blue eyes did not flicker as he turned away but he had noticed Brenda toss her long, brown hair back, though whether in anger or disappointment he wasn't sure.

*

126

Moira was watching the local evening news when she heard a crash. The murders were making her jumpy, more so because, apart from last night, Ian had been restless, disturbing her own sleep. The noise was, she knew, caused by a metal bucket she had left upside down on the back step to dry. The wind had blown it over. Not nervous by nature, she still glanced in both directions before she stepped out of the back door to retrieve it, mentally kicking herself. She had left the door unlocked, anyone could have simply walked in. The rain was coming down in stair-rods, then sweeping at an angle, taken by a gust of wind. It was the wettest winter in memory. Pools of water lay on the grass, the light from the kitchen window reflected in ripples and the borders were saturated. Only half the bulbs she had planted were appearing; she wondered if the rest had drowned.

Had those other women left their doors open? she wondered as she secured it behind her. No, surely Mrs Baxter would have been more careful. And where was Ian? He hadn't telephoned. Two chicken breasts were ready in the fridge, she would start supper anyway. In the slits she made Moira placed a slice of smoked bacon and a slice of cheese, then coated them in the parsley butter she kept in the freezer. If Ian was late the vegetables would also come from the freezer.

He rang as she was lighting the oven. He *was* going to be late. Feeling restless and in need of company she rang Deirdre. Deidre was thirty when she became a widow but had never remarried, saying a suitable replacement had not materialised. However, she was still not ruling out the possibility as she was only a year or two older than Moira. Their friendship had survived over the years. Moira had not met the husband but had seen his photographs which lined the mantelpiece. They must have been a constant reminder to Deirdre and possibly put off any viable suitor.

'I'm glad you asked,' Deirdre said. 'I haven't got any meetings tonight and there's nothing on the box.'

'How flattering,' Moira replied as she let her in. 'I hope you haven't eaten?'

'No, but I suppose I'm here to eat what the DCI won't be here to eat. Talk about waste not want not. I guessed as much. Here. Wrong colour but I don't suppose you care.' She produced a bottle of Chianti from her capacious handbag. 'Oh, and that book you lent me.'

Moira handed her the corkscrew. 'You know where the glasses are. Peas or mange-tout?' she asked as she measured rice into the saucepan.

By the time they had drunk their first glass of wine the meal was ready. 'Something happened today which really touched me.'

'Oh?'

'The Guild sent me the most beautiful bouquet and a lovely card to thank me for fifteen years' service on the committee. It's lovely to know your efforts are appreciated.'

'You deserve it.' And she did. Deirdre put her heart into all she did. Moira put her knife and fork down.

'Moira?'

'The flowers. I take it they were delivered by a florist, not one of the Guild?'

'Of course they were.' Deirdre frowned. 'Why?'

'How? No, what I mean is, did you just open the door without thinking?

'You're talking about these murders, aren't you? Yes, I did actually, but I'm no silly young thing, Moira, look at me. I doubt if anyone would question it if I applied for a bus pass. I'm not implying that those other women were silly, but they were attractive. Besides, the delivery man was a woman.'

'Honestly, Deirdre.' But Moira had to admit her friend did look older than her years although it was a face age would be kind to because Deirdre had not altered in all the time Moira had known her.

Deirdre was doing her own bit of stocktaking. Moira, in jeans and shirt and sweatshirt, the make-up washed from her face and her hair tied back, could pass for ten years younger. Life was not terribly fair at times. 'And another thing. I saw the van arrive from the window and the girl was coming up my path so I had to assume the flowers were for me.'

'Exactly.'

'Surely Ian's checked all that sort of thing?'

'Yes, he must have. Come on, finish up this rice, there's not enough to do anything else with.'

Deirdre had only been gone a few minutes when Ian came home. 'Smells nice,' he said, causing Moira a quick pang of guilt for giving away his meal. She defrosted a chop in the microwave while he hung up his coat and sat down at the kitchen table with a cigarette and a half-pint glass of Adnams poured from the two-litre plastic container she had bought in the supermarket. 'I didn't intend being late tonight but I took the afternoon off then went back in.'

'What on earth did you do with yourself?' There was a total absence of signs that he had sat in some pub or other.

'I went to the pictures.'

'You didn't? What did you see?'

'Something called *Natural Born Killers*.'

'Oh, Ian.'

'What's so funny?'

But she did not tell him that the last thing she would have wanted to watch was a violent film about murder if she was taking half a day away from three real ones. She turned the chop under the grill and served it with runner beans and potato croquettes from the freezer. He did not seem to notice any discrepancy between what he had smelled and what he was eating. But that was not unusual, he was frequently less than observant in his own house.

When he had eaten she brought up the idea of it being a florist's delivery van who had gone to all three addresses. He listened, Moira was no fool, then shook his head. 'We've turned over every damned florist in this town and beyond. Markham went over it again today as well because Carrie Griffiths had a birthday recently. But you're right, Moira, I'm still convinced it has to be something like that.' The problem was, what?

It was not the time to speak to Ian about the changes she wanted to make in her own life. Instead, Moira filled a bowl with water and washed his few dishes.

'Same old story. Dr Patterson said there was no reason why she couldn't have children, she was a healthy young woman, although she ignored his advice to give up smoking if she was intending to start a family. The only recent visit to the surgery was for an infected finger which she wanted to clear up quickly because she hated wearing gloves in the salon.'

'And Brian Griffiths?'

'He's not registered anywhere, says he doesn't trust the medical profession.'

'Neither do I when I'm on the receiving end.' Ian added to the further disintegration to the end of his biro by chewing it. 'And I still think your original idea about them being childless is relevant, but God knows in what way.'

'We've started to get one or two complaints, you know. A couple of the local businesses aren't too pleased about repeated visits from the CID.'

'Funny, isn't it – when they get broken into they complain we're never around.'

Carrie Griffiths' list of friends and acquaintances was large. She had lived all her life in Rickenham and there were old school friends, her brothers' friends and girlfriends and all the people with whom she came into contact at work. It was taking a long time to see them all. The Chief had to content himself with letting the various teams get on with it while he began sorting out the numerous pieces of paper which were littering his desk. Paperwork took up a larger percentage of his time than he would have wished but it was part of the price he had paid for promotion. At twelve thirty he suggested to Barry that they go out and get something to eat.

As they sat in the small café with toasted sandwiches and pottery mugs of coffee on the table in front of them, Ian thought over what Moira had said and related the conversation to Barry. 'We know there's no record to coincide with that but there's another way of looking at it.'

'Which is?' Barry winced as boiling, melted cheese burned his mouth.

'Delivery vans are inconspicuous simply because of what they are, just like men digging up the road – you know they're there, but you don't really see them. And if you've got a job like that you get around, you get to know things. Sometimes parcels have to be left with neighbours, and neighbours talk, and I don't know why it is but the recipients feel obliged to give an explanation. I heard Moira do it not long ago. Our postman couldn't get a package through the letter-box and she tells him it's a book she ordered, some special offer or something. The same with flowers, I'll bet you anything you like women make comments – you know, I can't think who they're from, it isn't my birthday. Just imagine how many small pieces of information you could pick up in a day.'

'Fair enough, but how does that help us?'

'Goddamn it all, Barry, it's there, it's in there somewhere amongst what we've been saying. I'm just thinking aloud and you're sitting there getting as pedantic as Campbell.'

Barry smiled engagingly at the woman at the next table, who had been trying to listen to their conversation but only managed to properly hear the final outburst. With a sniff of disgust she turned her attention back to the meringue she was struggling with as crumbs flew everywhere.

Smithy had not taken any time off since he had started the new job, one which the benefits office had no knowledge of. He asked for, and was given, a day off. He wanted a glimpse of his wife – his ex-wife – whom he had found easily enough despite the unlisted telephone number. What he hoped to see was an expression of misery on her pretty little face; despair in her eyes until she saw him, then they would light up and she would see how wrong she had been to leave him. And the baby ... that was something which was quite beyond him. Of

131

course, they must have adopted it. There was nothing on the back of the photograph, he did not even know what sex it was.

He had not dared ask around, to use his expertise in Rickenham, but he had found her and was secretly proud of the way in which he had done so.

Des, now her husband, was a plumber and he had known him slightly in their Leicester days. When Sheila left him he heard the rumours, that it was Des with whom she had gone. He waited, Sheila would come back, come crawling back, begging his forgiveness, and he would take her back, except she would be made to pay for it. But he had been wrong and the finality of it only sank in when he received a letter from her solicitors.

Des was no cowboy, he must belong to one of the institutes. A couple of telephone calls confirmed this and he was given his work address.'It's in the book, you know,' the man at the other end told him.

And so, when he received that photograph, he knew he had to find them. He had laughed, how naïve they must be, Sheila and Des. There had been nothing else in the envelope, only the snapshot, probably taken in hospital, his ex-wife sitting up in bed holding the baby. It had been posted at King's Cross, London, but that hadn't fooled him, they had got someone else to post it.

Marian had been a temporary distraction, for sex – he needed sex, he needed a woman to clean and cook, and he thought he had found one. He thought Marian's reticence was because she was a decent girl, the sort that didn't sleep around and would therefore cause him no worries. But that was in the past.

The weather was not unpleasant. He drove to the outskirts of the town and cruised around, wanting to be certain. There, down behind the disused goods yard at the back of the railway station, were several small units, businesses which were too small to be able to afford to move to the Poplars Business Park. Des Cowan's name was painted on a board over one of them. He had parked quite close, there was no need to hide – the car would not be recognised and he was certainly not expected.

Just after five Des arrived, driving a pick-up truck which he parked in the yard. Smithy watched from behind the wheel of his own vehicle. The twenty minutes until his quarry re-appeared dragged. 'You bastard,' he hissed, 'you adulterous, fucking bastard.' With great self-restraint he remained in the car. He had not known how much he hated Des and in that moment could have killed him. No, Des's suffering would be greater if *he* survived and his wife didn't. Smithy was going to take Sheila away from him just as the reverse was once true.

Des sauntered across the yard, truck keys swinging from his fingers. Smithy waited until he had pulled out into the road before he turned the ignition. He lowered the sun visor and allowed a car to intercept them. It was not long before Des indicated left and turned into a cul-de-sac where he parked, locked the driver's door and went round to the back to remove a tool-box. Unaware that he was being observed, Des walked up the short path of a small, modern house and inserted his key in the front door.

Smithy grinned. So that's where they lived. Strange, not once had he come across either of them in the street, and he got around a bit, but life was like that.

It had been a bonus to be allowed to borrow the boss's car. He knew the van would be needed so had not bothered to ask but the car needed an MOT. He was offered the use of it provided he took it in for its test, which he had done early that morning. He had said he wanted to go to Oxford to visit his cousin. The cousin had moved, but that didn't matter, and he had destroyed the letter with the new address.

His body almost tingled with satisfaction as he reversed into a side road and turned the car around. Now he had it, he might as well make the most of it and have a run out into the country, or even down to the coast. It would be dark, but he hadn't seen the sea since he arrived. He got on the ring road and followed the signs for Aldeburgh.

8

The third inquest had gone as smoothly as the previous two and Carrie's family were free to make their arrangements. A discreet police presence had been maintained at the burial and cremation services of the other victims, and the same would apply here. It was not uncommon for a murderer to turn up for whatever macabre reason.

In the intervening days since Carrie's death it was ascertained that no cab firm had taken or collected a passenger to or from any of the relevant addresses. A negative, but at least an elimination.

'It's unnerving,' Barry said. He and Ian knew all the latest theories on the habits of serial killers, the predominant trait being that the times between crimes lessened as the urge to repeat them became stronger. 'There hasn't been another one.'

'For God's sake, don't tempt fate.'

'You're not superstitious.'

'I didn't use to be.'

They were seated in postures which were becoming more common with each passing day, slumped in an attitude which hinted at defeat. There were rings from coffee cups and a dirty ashtray on the desk. They had shut the door and opened the window in order to smoke. Ian closed it now and retrieved some papers which had blown to the floor in the draught. The cold did not bother them; only the murders mattered.

'Do you think there's any significance in the fact that it's three?'

'You mean will he stop now? I doubt it, Barry, not unless

he had a specific reason for killing these particular women.'
And they both knew that likelihood had been ruled out. 'He
has transport, or access to transport, and I'm still inclined to
think it's something anonymous. I don't necessarily mean
unmarked, but something no one looks at twice, the sort of
thing where no one is going to question the authenticity of the
driver.'

'So someone who might not deliver, but has the use of a
van? No, the women were killed during working hours.'

DC Alan Campbell had even come up with a couple of men
who had travelling shops, a method of dealing Barry thought
no longer existed. They had not been patronised by the
victims. Brian and Carrie Griffiths had a pizza home delivery
during the week prior to her death. This information had only
come to light because, although there was no record of it, the
youth whose job it was to take it had said he did not fancy the
idea of going to Magnolia House at ten thirty at night on his
scooter. The boss had lent him the car. 'They're an easy target,
these lads, nowadays,' he said. 'They get paid in cash and in
that area there's every chance of them being mugged. They
see the bike and wait for them to come out. With an ordinary
car they don't realise what's going on and I can't afford to lose
a customer, not with two other pizza places in the town now.'

Debbie Orchard believed in healthy eating and although
Roy said they occasionally had a Chinese take-away he went
out for it himself as it was only a ten-minute walk. The
Baxters, if not eating at home, went out to restaurants. The
pizza delivery boy had been terrified when he was questioned
but, it turned out, without reason to be.

'All right, supposing you're new to a job like that, you've
got to learn your way around. You get provided with a street
map, but look . . .' Ian opened an *A-Z* of Rickenham Green
and pointed to the fold where it was almost impossible to
read the street names, especially the back streets. 'And here.'
He flipped over a page. Even in the middle of a page a
magnifying glass would have been needed to read it clearly.
'So what do you do? You ask.'

'If you're in Broomhill Lane which isn't signed, like a lot of those places – but Alexander Road? No, you'd go to the paper shop, and you can't seriously believe someone traipsed up to the third floor of Magnolia House to ask directions?'

'Suggest something better.' Ian was truculent. Barry was right but he wasn't the one having his ideas shot to pieces. 'Sod it, I'm going out.'

He was not a big drinker but a decent meal was called for to celebrate. There must be some seafood restaurants on the coast.

Walking along the sand in the dark with the gentle lapping of the waves to soothe him, Smithy felt at peace for the first time since he could remember. There was no rush now, that sense of urgency tightening his chest had gone. He stood on the shoreline and threw pebbles into the sea, and listened to the satisfying plop as they hit the water and disappeared for ever. Just as Sheila would.

DS Swan stared gloomily down at the street below. He had just spent an hour with a man who had walked into the station and claimed responsibility for all three murders. He sounded plausible, giving the correct addresses, describing the women and saying he had seen them in town and followed them home. Once he knew where they lived he had returned later and knocked on their doors then strangled them because he hated all women. He said he wore gloves. He drew an accurate plan of Carrie's flat and provided a very close description of the house in Alexander Road. But something wasn't quite right and Barry was already beginning to have his doubts, although he pressed on anyway. Only when it came to the description of the Baxters' house did he fall down.

What had confused DS Swan and DC Campbell was that the man had all the appearance of a confessing criminal, from the sweat on his upper lip to the half-fearful, half-victorious pose he adopted. Once the flaw had been discovered, it was only a matter of time before they sent him on his way again.

'Been in before?' Alan Campbell asked.

'Not one of our usual nutters.' And this time there had been relatively few, perhaps because it was harder to convince someone of your guilt if three incidents were involved. Such confessions were more common than most people might think, although why innocent citizens wanted to hold up their hands to something they didn't do was a frequent topic of conversation. Sometimes it was to draw attention away from the real culprit, occasionally to gain some form of recognition, however grisly, but mostly it was a gesture of loneliness.

That hour of wasted time had to be paid for, the details typed up, the statement nullified – another chore to add to the ever-increasing frustration.

Markham spent the afternoon working on building up a complete picture of the Johns family. Simon was not the only one to have been in trouble. Mr Johns, in his younger days, had not been averse to selling property which did not belong to him, but the information provided by Felixstowe, from where Mr Johns came, included no record of violence. Markham was now trying to find out what had happened to the villains with whom he had mixed in case they had gone on to bigger things. Perhaps, as Simon knew Damien Marsh, the family had wittingly, or unwittingly, provided someone with details they had put to use.

'Where's the Chief?' he wanted to know.

'Out,' DC Gibbons told him. 'Why?'

'Because William Johns was once in partnership with Monroe O'Sullivan before he went on to bigger things.' Brenda Gibbons looked puzzled. 'Before your time. O'Sullivan progressed to violence and finally killed his wife; he got away with manslaughter. His brief put up a good defence, said he'd suffered unendurable provocation, and even the wife's family admitted she was bad news.'

'And he's out?'

'Yep.'

'How come we didn't know about it?'

'Because, according to his probation officer, he's now living in Leeds, but she knows he's trying to get in touch with some of his old mates and she doesn't think it's simply out of friendship.'

It was a long shot. Had Damien Marsh inadvertently boasted about his wealthy neighbours to Simon? Simon also knew Mrs Orchard from school, and Carrie was his sister. Had Simon, or one of the family, passed this information on for some reason or another? O'Sullivan was unemployed and only had to report to his probation officer on a weekly basis, he had plenty of spare time.

'But not Carrie,' Brenda said decisively. 'They don't usually turn on their own kind.'

'Johns isn't one of his own kind, he was a petty thief and a fence. O'Sullivan preferred a bit of the rough stuff. And he killed his own wife, you can't get closer to home than that.'

Markham contacted his counterparts in Leeds, who were later rewarded for their efforts by a complaint of police harassment from Monroe O'Sullivan.

Ian had not spoken personally to the inhabitants of Magnolia House. The idea still lingered that Brian Griffiths could have killed his wife before leaving for work. The estimated time of death was between 7 and 9 a.m. on that Wednesday morning, which was as near as anyone could ever get, and if they had had a row there was no one to hear it. The lorry driver opposite had been away and Mrs Bennett, in the flat next door, had been staying with her brother, having set off that morning early. Ian wanted to jog her memory. Just how early? Surely not before seven. And although she had already been asked, she was elderly – her memory might play tricks, and the elderly were better at remembering distant things than present ones, not that a matter of a couple of weeks was distant. Had she conceivably passed someone on the stairs as she left?

On the grass outside Magnolia House a couple of children kicked a ball in a desultory manner. They were aged about ten or eleven and Ian wondered why they were not at school, it wasn't half-term, but then, he reasoned, not many around here cared much about their children's education. He was in the sort of mood where he disliked the whole world and most of the people in it – Moira being the exception. Magnolia House, he thought, was just as gloomy in the wintry sun as on a wet and miserable day.

Dustbins and bulging plastic sacks were stacked alongside the building. It was bin day. Had this area been on Brian Griffiths' route, did he empty his own bin? No, he remembered now – they had checked because it might have given him an opportunity to slip indoors. The council offices had supplied enough details for them to know that three different lorries, three different sets of men, were responsible for collecting the rubbish from the roads in which the victims had lived.

Outside, lounging against the wall, a man stood smoking a small cigar. When the children's ball came towards him he kicked it back, looking very much as if he would like to join in. Ian said good morning and was surprised when he received a grunted acknowledgement by way of a reply. He mounted the stairs and stood in the corridor outside flat number 11. Brian Griffiths had moved in with his sister; he had vowed never to return.

A smell of frying food drifted from under the door opposite, the lorry driver's residence, but it was not a pleasant smell: the fat had burned at some stage and was being reused. The lorry driver was not worth another visit. He had been on a cross-Channel ferry at the time of Carrie's death, and when Debbie Orchard met her untimely end he had been in Devon attending his grandmother's funeral.

Ian shook his head. Nothing, no feelings, no hunches. He tapped on the door of number 10 and waited a long time before it was answered. He had almost given up when he heard rustling noises behind it.

'I hope I'm not disturbing you,' he said to the half of a face he could see between the frame and the side of the door. He slanted his identification at an angle so it could be seen.

'No, not at all, just a minute.' The door closed then was reopened as Mrs Bennett took the chain off. She was blushing. 'I don't get around as quickly as I used to,' she said, hoping this man would not realise that she had been using the bathroom and that it took her a while to do the necessary and wash her hands. 'Come in, please.'

She reiterated how upset she had been to hear the news but underneath Ian saw how pleased she was to have company, even if it was yet another policeman. For that reason he accepted the offer of a cup of tea.

Whilst she went to make it in the small kitchen, almost identical to the one next door, he noticed that although few of the objects in the room were new, they were well cared for. The table, of a size to seat two, was scratched but polished so he was not surprised when the tea came to see it served on a tray with milk in a jug and some biscuits on a plate.

'I'm old, Chief Inspector,' she told him when he began his questions, 'but I'm not senile. I have thought and thought about it ever since. I left here at seven forty on that Wednesday morning and I didn't hear a thing next door. Brian must have left because he starts at eight and he has to get the bus into town, and I know it was that time because my bus left at five to and it takes me ten minutes to get to the stop. And before that, no strangers've been up here to my knowledge. Go on,' she saw the direction of his glance, 'have it.' Ian picked up the last chocolate digestive. 'In fact, no one comes up here much except the postman and he doesn't get here until around eleven. I once took in a parcel for Mr Singh and the postman stuck a note through his door to say I'd got it so I knew it was all right. He's gone now. Mr Singh, I mean, not the postman. Dear me, I do sound muddled. I miss him, he was a nice man for all his turban. This new one, he looks dirty to me, still he's quiet enough.' Mrs Bennett sipped her tea, hoping she did not sound senile.

'You knew Carrie well enough for her to do your hair so I expect you know she had a birthday not long before she died?'

'Yes. I put a card through the door.'

'Now, I know you've been asked this before, but would you be aware of anyone delivering anything on that day, parcels, or flowers or anything?'

Mrs Bennett shook her head. 'No. As I said, the post comes late. If she had a parcel they must have taken it back to the sorting office for her to collect later. That was a Wednesday, too, wasn't it?'

There was obviously nothing wrong with the lady's memory.

'Oh, my goodness.' Her hands trembled as she placed the cup and saucer back on the tray.

'Mrs Bennett?'

She stared at Ian with horror. 'Oh, how stupid of me.'

'You've remembered something?'

'Yes. On her birthday, no one came, not that I saw, but I did see her going to work from the window. Oh, Chief Inspector, whatever will you think of me? She was carrying a bouquet, roses, they were, done up in cellophane.'

'It's all right, really, please don't upset yourself.' And although it might mean nothing – Carrie might have bought them to give to someone and wrapped them herself to save money – that thing that had been missing throughout the whole case was suddenly there. A gut feeling, instinct, call it whatever you like – Ian knew this was it. Women, he suspected, did not generally choose roses as a gift; mixed flowers, yes, but not roses. 'You've no idea how helpful you've been, Mrs Bennett, and thank you for the tea.'

She blushed at the praise. 'There's more in the pot.'

'It's very kind of you but I have to get back.'

'Call in any time you're in the neighbourhood,' she said as he left, reaffirming her loneliness.

From somewhere or other Carrie Griffiths had acquired those flowers and, at least according to her husband, they had not been in the flat the previous evening. His mind was racing as he drove back. Had she gone out and purchased them then returned to wrap them? If so, where? No, came the conflicting assumption, and it was too much of a coincidence to believe this had happened when it was *her* birthday. Moira, it seemed, had been on the right track although he wasn't sure yet in which direction it was going.

The euphoria was draining away by the time he had parked and made his way to the control room. She must have bought them otherwise there would be a delivery record at one of the flower shops.

'Florists,' he said. 'How many men can be spared?' The officers working their way solidly through statements stared at him open-mouthed as if he had gone mad. They had checked each and every one of them twice. 'Forget everything else, this is important. I want someone immediately in every shop and I want to find out who sent Carrie Griffiths a bouquet of roses on her birthday. We've now got a definite date to work from.' Please, God, he thought, let Mrs Bennett be right, let her not have confused the days. He called an emergency briefing then went to find Barry.

'Something's happened.' Ian's mood was very different from when Barry had last seen him.

'Maybe. Come on, we're going for a pint. It was a little early for celebrations and drinking in the middle of the day was frowned upon, yet once he had given his instructions he was sure this was it.

'Now?'

'Yes, now.' He would have liked to see the florists individually himself but feared he was too prejudiced. If you expected to find something, there was always the inclination to make something out of nothing; it was better to delegate. 'It is lunchtime.'

'Lunchtime? It's nearly three o'clock.'

'My lunchtime then. That can wait.' He indicated the files on the desk.

It would take at least an hour before he knew anything, and he could not bear to spend it sitting in an office. How wonderful if, by the time he went home that evening, it was all over.

But it was not to be.

They were to remain in their same squads, Markham heading the team who would once more be upsetting local traders, DC Campbell back on the door knocking. He was with the officers in Alexander Road as they worked outwards from the Orchards' house. At the end of the road they would cross over and work their way in the opposite direction.

The first house, to the left, Campbell took himself. 'A man can't read the bloody paper in peace these days. Haven't you found him yet?' was the initial, unenthusiastic response. And so it went on. Some houses were unoccupied and those people who were at home had already told the police what they knew and resented a further interruption. Although Mrs Orchard's death was still a conversation piece, the horror was beginning to recede, they had their own lives to get on with.

And then, five doors down, a Mrs Ingram, with a flushed-faced, teething infant on her hip, remembered. 'Not me,' she said, 'no one ever sends me flowers. Beth Abbott had some though. What's it got to do with the murder?'

'It's just a lead we're following,' Alan Campbell told her. 'Where does Beth Abbott live?'

'Number 19. Lived. She's not there any more.' This was not what he needed to hear. 'What happened was Beth's husband sent her the flowers on their wedding anniversary. She was furious – he was away at the time and she said that it was an afterthought, and that if he wanted to he could easily have come home that night. Turns out she was right, there was another woman. Anyway, Beth says she's had enough, it wasn't the first time apparently, and off she goes, back to her mother's. *He's* still there.' She nodded in the direction of the house. 'And I know what I'd do if I was married to him.' Alan continued to listen. Mrs Abbott may have gone but flowers had been delivered in this road.

143

'How long ago was this, Mrs Ingram?'

'Dunno. Five, six weeks ago.'

Perfect. 'I don't suppose you know which florist it was?'

'No. Be quiet for five minutes,' she said to the child. 'He's driving me mad. The only one who might've known is Debbie. Sad, isn't it, but that's life, I suppose.'

'Debbie Orchard?'

'Yes. Beth was out when they came and Debbie was just coming home from work – she offered to take them in and give them to Beth later.'

'How do you know this?'

'Because Beth told me, when she came round to have a moan about that no-good husband of hers.'

Alan was beginning to see why the Chief had been so insistent. Two out of three women had had flowers in their house just prior to their deaths. 'Why didn't you mention this to anyone before?'

'Why should I? It was Debbie you lot were interested in. I can't see what Beth Abbott getting flowers from her husband's got to do with anything.'

He had to concede the point. 'Mrs Ingram, I – '

'Honestly, I've tried to do my bit, we all have in Alexander Road, like it says in the Neighbourhood Watch thing, but it seems you just can't do enough at times.'

'No offence meant. Thank you for your time.'

He might as well let the others continue; who knew what else might come to light? He gave DC Gibbons a friendly wave and left after he said he was going to report his discovery to the Chief in person.

'One of our regulars?' Ian asked when Barry had told him about the false confession.

'No. Turns out he used to live in Magnolia House, shared a flat with someone there for a couple of months, hence the accurate description, and his mother used to live in a terraced place so he had a rough idea what the possible layout would be.'

'Come on, let's get back.' They had only been out for half an hour but Ian was restless. He merely nodded when Alan Campbell gave an outline of what Mrs Ingram had told him. His hunch was looking more like a certainty and when Markham rang in at four forty his optimism soared.

'I'm at Petals, sir,' he said. 'Opposite the town hall.'

Ian knew it. The new town hall was housed in a pedestrianised area, surrounded by modern office blocks, the buildings forming three sides of a square. In the middle was a fountain and there were raised flower beds and a few trees to break up the urban monotony. On the other side of the road the buildings had been modernised and now formed a row of rather bijou shops and boutiques, including Petals.

'Why wasn't it noticed?' He made a note to reprimand those responsible then crossed it out when he heard Markham's explanation.

'The order was addressed to Caroline Johns and the address given was 11 Waveney Road. However, the shop received a telephone call the morning after the order was received to say it was 11 Magnolia House, Waveney Road, and as the driver was just loading the van, he was given the new directions verbally. The manager had forgotten all about it until I queried it. Waveney Road was the nearest address to anything for the date of the birthday.'

Ian knew his annoyance was unreasonable. Why should the manager or owner have been expected to recall one delivery out of hundreds, especially when the name was not the one they had been looking for and they were initially checking deliveries over a period of several weeks, not one day. Caroline Johns. So someone either did not know she was married or had forgotten her new name. In which case, who was the mystery person? Everyone they had interviewed so far had been aware of her marital state.

Before Markham rang off he said the driver they wanted to

speak to had taken the day off but the manager had provided his home address.

'And he's got the manager's car?'

'Yes, sir.'

'OK, you'd better come back.' If Robert Smith had borrowed the boss's car he was not likely to do a bunk. He would be too easy to find.

'You're jumping to conclusions,' Superintendent Thorne told him when he repeated this sentiment. 'And you don't know yet if Mrs Abbott's flowers came from the same shop.'

'We shall, as soon as DS Markham returns.'

'All right. Send someone over to pick him up.'

But Robert Smith was not at home.

It was the first time Markham had been inside Petals; he was not a man who ever bought flowers. The bell on the door chimed and a fresh-faced girl in an overall and boots came from somewhere at the back of the shop. She smiled pleasantly and asked if he knew what he was looking for.

'It's the manager I'd like to see,' he said. 'Police.'

The girl nodded and went to fetch him. It was the third visit they had had.

A tall, balding man who, upon closer scrutiny, was far younger than Markham first took him for came forward and shook his hand, an action which surprised him. Roger Walker,' he said. 'We haven't seen you before. Come through here, we can talk in my office. Be careful of the floor.'

The shop was artfully arranged but the scent of flowers was overpowering, cloying and sickly. The rear area was cold and he saw why the girl wore boots: the floor, where stems had been removed from buckets of water, was wet. It was also slippery; blackened leaves and bits of stalks were left to lie where they fell after being cut. Two doors stood open on to a patch of concrete where the vans pulled in to be loaded with the bouquets and baskets and arrangements the girl and one other female were putting together with speed and skill before

146

wrapping them in cellophane and decorating them with loops and bows or thin, curly streamers made by running the blade of a pair of scissors along a length of ribbon.

Markham was slightly puzzled, he had expected a more antagonistic reception, but he was unaware that Roger Walker's life was dull and that their visits added a touch of excitement, even glamour to the day and gave him something to talk to his wife about.

'Sharon,' Walker called, 'would you do two coffees, please? I take it you'd like some?' he added to his guest.

'Thanks, black with no sugar.'

Walker's office was much warmer than anywhere else on the premises, heated by a one-bar electric fire mounted on the wall. It was hardly more than a box-room but was adequate for his purposes.

'It's no skin off my nose how many times you come back. I don't know why people get so uptight about it. How else do they think you can solve crimes?' Walker accepted Markham's apology for a further interruption graciously. 'And if you've got nothing to hide, there's no problem. Ah, coffee. Thanks, love. Are the table arrangements ready for the Masonic do? Good. I'll take them myself later.'

'I'd like another look at your order books if you don't mind.'

'Certainly. The old ones are here.' He indicated a shelf to his right. 'I'll just get the one we're on now.' It was under the counter in the shop. Markham began going through the pages of the one he realised was for the relevant date and found what he wanted fairly quickly. Walker could not have been expected to know Carrie's maiden name was Johns and none of them had had the gumption to look for that name. And the address was inaccurate.

In the previous book was the order for Beth Abbott, the message reading 'Happy Anniversary, love Reg.' This was not important, it only confirmed that it had been an anniversary – what was important was that Debbie Orchard and Carrie Griffiths were now inseparably linked. The message that would have been written on Carrie's card was more cryptic:

'Too late the hero. Don.' He got Walker to trace the origins of the sender.

'According to the shop in Manchester, a Don Gilbert sent them. This is his address. Is it him? Is that who killed her?'

Markham evaded answering. He did not want to give Walker a chance to warn their suspect, which he might do without meaning to, so he changed tack and asked general questions about drivers and their methods of operation. Walker supplied the information without being aware he was doing so.

'Smithy would've delivered them. I have to keep a record as the two men we employ get paid by the delivery.'

'And these?' Markham pointed to a name which meant nothing, then two more, before indicating Beth Abbott's address.

'Pete. Pete again, then the next two were Smithy's.'

'I'll need to speak to both men.'

Walker wrote down their home addresses and was thanked by Markham, who walked sedately out of the shop giving Sharon a lingering smile on the way. Smithy, it appeared, was paid cash in hand.

'It's the first day off he's had since he started,' he told Ian. 'He's not expected back at the shop tonight but he's taking the car in in the morning.'

'We've got someone watching his place. He's not in.' The make and registration number of the car were now a matter of record in the unlikely event Robert Smith did not come back.

'Do we know why he wanted the day off?'

'To see his cousin in Oxford, or so he says.'

There had been another link between the first and third victims – they had both been killed on a Wednesday, which pointed to the possibility that Wednesday was the killer's day off – but this did not apply to Virginia Baxter. As all three crimes were committed on weekdays, during normal working hours, it might be that their man was unemployed or worked shifts. Then they began to see that the murders might have been committed whilst the man was working, and that he would need transport and a job that kept him out and about. And now, Ian was sure, they had him. What they did not have was a connection with Ginny Baxter. Emma Dearing had been seen again: she swore no flowers had come, and there had been none in the house on the day of Ginny's death other than some Emma herself had purchased and arranged upon her employer's instructions.

'I hope he turns up soon,' Ian said, referring to Smith. They had no photograph but Walker had given a clear enough description to make him recognisable.

Leaving it all in other, capable hands, Ian, Barry, Alan Campbell and Brenda Gibbons made their way up the High Street in a mood reminiscent of being let out of school early although it was after six thirty. The evenings were drawing out and some light remained in the sky; the moon, nearly full, floated behind a cloud and reappeared, even brighter. A ground frost was forecast, which everyone was saying would help kill off the germs causing so many head colds. They waited, in an orderly fashion, for the pedestrian lights to change in their favour, joking, making remarks that could only be understood by anyone in the job.

'The Feathers it is, then,' Ian agreed, going along with the consensus of opinion because the burden had been lifted; by the time his head was on his pillow tonight the murderer would be in the cells. He watched, amused, as Alan made small talk to the delectable DC Gibbons, her long hair gleaming under the lights as they stood at the bar, her green eyes echoing what Ian felt. Alan Campbell was no match for Brenda but at least he was taking an interest in women again after his disastrous marriage and a drawn-out divorce.

'You've got him,' Moira said as soon as she saw his face.

'As good as.' He slapped her playfully, but rather too enthusiastically, on the bottom. She flinched. 'Any phone calls?'

'No.'

'Mm.' Moira would have told him immediately – she was very conscientious about doing so, no matter how much she might resent his having to go out again. In his pocket was his mobile phone. That had been silent all evening too. He took it out and plugged it in to charge up overnight. Still, it was only ten. If Smith had borrowed the car, presumably he had a longish journey to make; he might not get home until the small hours, which would not please whoever was on observation. Ian wanted to be informed when they had him, no more than that. His obsession was not with interviewing the suspect, it was with catching him. Someone else, anyone else, could take the confession statement. Statement, he reminded himself, it might not be a confession. Worse, it might not be Smith who had killed them. He refused to allow pessimism to spoil the last couple of hours. It had been one of those evenings which gelled perfectly. Seated in his armchair, the flower-patterned suite soothing in its familiarity, he watched the news while Moira dished up their meal. He smiled; he had always liked the fact that, whenever possible, she waited to eat with him.

A little after midnight they went to bed. The telephone had not rung once.

9

By the time he pulled off the dual carriageway Smithy's eyes felt gritty and he wondered if he might need glasses. He would look into it, but not yet, not until he had killed Sheila. The anticipation was almost as good as the deed itself and maybe, just maybe, he'd sort out that bitch Marian as well.

Aldeburgh had been disappointing, not the place itself, but because he could not find anywhere suitable to eat. Restaurants were closed for the winter and the hotel dining-room was fully booked. It was just as well in a way because he could not really afford it and it was nicer to get home, not to have a drive ahead after he had eaten.

The lights of Rickenham Green were a welcome sight because he was exhausted, mentally more than physically. He was not going to cook for himself now, a chore he bitterly resented when there should be a woman to do it. He would have a kebab or something. Yes, a kebab, he had not had one for ages. He had to pass Petals so it would be simpler to leave the car there. With all the driving he now did, he was not as fit as he liked to be and, besides, he might as well have several drinks. It would be the one and only time he would allow himself to be out of control; not drunk, far from that, but relaxed and mellow.

He pulled into the yard behind the shop and locked the car, checking all four doors. Roger Walker would not take too kindly to his car being stolen through his carelessness. Crossing the road, he decided to take his chances in the Prince William; from there it was no distance to the take-away and only a few minutes' walk home. He settled for a single drink, a bottle of brown ale, then purchased his food. Whistling to himself he made his way back to the two-bedroomed semi he was renting cheaply. It was on the Bradley Court housing estate in a quiet road where the neighbours kept mostly to themselves.

As soon as he rounded the corner he sensed something was wrong. He stood very still, unable to decide what it was. The hairs on the nape of his neck bristled, he was in danger, but his training had stood him in good stead. Sheltered by the shadow of the wall which curved around the corner of the end house, he rapidly surveyed the scene. To anyone else it would appear normal, not so to Smithy. There was no one about, which was unexceptional – people here tended not to go out during the week and watched television. He listened. A baby cried nearby, its plaintive wail a thin sound coming from an upstairs window where a light appeared behind the drawn curtains. There was the muffled sound of traffic in the distance and the roar of an engine as a car started up a street away.

The cars. That's what it was. He knew them all, knew exactly where each and every one of his neighbours parked and how they parked. They did exactly what he did if he ever took the van home; they drove to the end of the road where it widened, turned round and faced ready to drive out the next morning. It was easier to do it then than when everyone seemed to be setting off at the same time. Because there were no parking restrictions here and the road was well lit, there were no problems about parking facing the wrong way. He might be wrong, it might be that someone had a visitor, but there, on the left-hand side, was a car he did not recognise, one with the passenger door next to the pavement, and in the front, partially hidden by the back of the seat and the headrest, was a dark shape.

His stomach muscles contracted. He knew with certainty they were on to him and his mind froze with panic. What if he had decided to bring the car home after all? He could not have made a run for it, it was no match for a police car and he would not have put himself through the indignity of becoming involved in a chase only to be caught. He would have had to act as he must now: like a man with nothing to hide. His side felt warm and he realised he had been crushing the kebab in his anxiety. Grease had soaked through the paper and marked his clothing. That was the least of his worries.

The car. No one was watching the shop, not when he parked there. He wanted to laugh but smothered it. He was right, they were fools. He might not have been in the job for long but he knew enough to realise that driving beyond, and facing away from, the house you were observing was the best way to remain inconspicuous. You had the protection of the seat, the paleness of your face did not show up at night, and with the wing and rear-view mirrors angled correctly everything that was going on behind you could easily be seen. But they had made a mistake, they had assumed he would arrive in the car. Just because they had forgotten what their feet were for did not mean Smithy had – he had walked. There was no point in delaying it any longer. He had the car, he would kill Sheila tomorrow.

'Nothing, sir. Nobody all night.'

'OK. Thanks.' Ian dismissed the man who had been relieved on surveillance. The car that had been there during the night was gone; a police officer was now ensconced in the house opposite, the middle-aged occupant of which could not wait for it all to be over so she could tell her friends – not that she had any idea what was going on.

Walker had rung to say Robert Smith had not turned up for work and his car was still missing. Traffic Division were informed and told not to apprehend the driver but to contact the control room and take instructions from there. Ian was grinding his teeth. The blame lay with himself; it was his own short-sightedness which had given Smith the opportunity to flee and it was too late now for recriminations, he should have

153

got to him sooner. But he was still under the misapprehension that Smith had disappeared completely the previous day – he would have been even more infuriated to learn that he had returned and taken the car when no one was watching the back of Petals.

Discreet house-to-house inquiries were under way once more, this time in the region of Bradley Court although it was unlikely Smith would return to his own address now. DC Gibbons finally found a neighbour who knew him well enough to make any relevant comment. 'He's a strange sort of bloke,' she said, 'keeps very much to himself. Moody, too, and quite a temper if anyone parks in his space.'

'Parks? Does he have a car?'

'No, the van, the Petals van. He only spoke to me once, properly that is. I said if he wanted anything doing I'd be glad to help. He was on his own, see. He was quite rude, he said he had a wife who used to do all that sort of thing and she hadn't stayed so why should a stranger?'

'He's divorced?'

'He didn't say, but it seems like it.'

'Has he ever mentioned any children?'

'No, and I've never seen any. He'd get access, wouldn't he, if there were?'

'He didn't happen to mention his ex-wife's name?'

'No, sorry, can't help you there.'

No children. The phrase stuck in Brenda's mind, but his neighbour had not been certain, perhaps Smith just didn't bother with them.

She radioed the information in, mentioning that his attitude towards the woman she had spoken to suggested he might have been violent towards his ex-wife.

So there was a wife, Ian thought. 'When exactly did Marian Thomas make her complaint?'

Alan Campbell told him. 'But she dropped the charges. If she hadn't – '

'Precisely. Get her in again, we need to know as much as

154

possible about Smith and she's our only chance at the moment.'

Meanwhile the Manchester police, equipped with Don Gilbert's home address, were trying to get in touch with him. Could it be that the sender of those flowers was responsible after all? It seemed unlikely, especially as he had put his name to the card and his details were on record with the florist where he placed the order.

When, later that morning, there was still no sign of Smith, Superintendent Thorne, with difficulty, obtained a search warrant and detectives were sent to his house.

'Well, well,' DS Markham said, 'what do you make of this?' On the mantelpiece was an unframed Polaroid snapshot of a woman sitting up in bed holding a tiny baby. From the little that could be seen of the background, it seemed likely that it was taken in a hospital and that the baby was therefore newly born. What was more incongruous was that there were no other photographs in the house, no pictures on the walls and no ornaments of any description. That snapshot, then, meant a great deal.

A copy of it was transmitted to Leicester where it was confirmed that the woman was Sheila Smith, ex-wife of the man they were looking for. But the baby was not his. They had to find Sheila Smith or whatever her name was now. His guess was that if Smith was the killer she would be his next victim. He had already disappeared. They had to hope they were not too late.

Superintendent Thorne called a meeting. 'He oughtn't to get far if he's still driving,' he said. Technology had improved to such an extent that mini-computers in traffic patrol cars listed registrations of stolen vehicles, and a whole intricate network operated to show in which direction they were travelling once they had been spotted. 'We have a connection, but we must bear in mind that this is not conclusive evidence, although the circumstantial evidence is as follows.' He ticked off the items on his fingers. 'Smith had the opportunity and

155

he had transport – as already suggested, anonymous-looking transport.' The three vans belonging to Petals were white with a small logo on each side panel; the name and telephone number were painted on the back, but compared with their competitors their advertising was understated. 'He is known to be violent towards women, his wife has divorced him and has a child by another man, although this is only surmise because we do not know when that picture was taken. There's a chance she was pregnant when she left him, it could still be Smith's. It must also be borne in mind that we have nothing which pin-points his knowledge of the existence of Virginia Baxter, but I'm inclined to agree with Chief Inspector Roper and . . . yes?' The telephone interrupted him. 'Marian Thomas is downstairs.' It was also time for the meeting to disband.

DS Swan spoke to Marian, who was unable to add any more to what she had previously said. 'I've learned my lesson, I realise how stupid it is to go out with someone you know nothing about.' She was embarrassed to make this admission but did so anyway. Barry refused to tell her the reasons for her being questioned again and she returned to work in a puzzled frame of mind.

'Looking at it now, it seems like an admission.' Barry and Ian were aware that the term 'mechanic' was, or used to be, underworld slang for a hit-man or hired killer – not that they believed anyone was paying Smith.

'Is he that subtle? Perhaps he didn't want Mrs Thomas to know he drove a van for a living. God knows why, a job's a job. Of course, Walker'll have to pull his socks up.'

'No, he took it in good faith that Smith wasn't claiming anything and what he paid him was a pound short of what you can earn before tax.'

'Anyway, none of this matters, finding Smith is what matters. After that we can check up on any other little illegalities.'

They had received a fax from Manchester. Don Gilbert turned out to be a single man recently transferred to the city because of promotion and in temporary accommodation until he found somewhere to buy. Don Gilbert had been in love with Carrie during the period of her separation from Brian and had thought he stood a chance with her. He had heard, of course, that she was married and wished her well: because of his own good fortune and by way of a parting gift because he was starting a new life, he decided to send her some flowers for her birthday. He could not, he said, recall her husband's name but guessed Carrie Johns would find her. 'You know what it's like when you move,' he added. 'I'd lost the piece of paper with her address but I thought I'd remembered it correctly. I placed the order the day before then just as I was going to sleep I remembered I'd left a bit out. I rang them the next day.' Gilbert's firm alibied him for the dates of all three murders.

'Didn't want to make her husband jealous, I imagine.' The flowers must have been dumped or given away.

Ian chewed a thumbnail; it was midday and neither Smith nor the ex-Mrs Smith had been found.

Smithy had approached the car through the scrubby bushes which divided the parking area from a piece of wasteland, ditching the cold kebab on the way. He took his time, making sure he was not being watched. Soon, possibly very soon, someone would realise their mistake and come to the shop but hopefully they would be watching the roads they expected him to be on, ones leading back from Oxford. Meanwhile, he was headed in the opposite direction. There was still a chance, as long as he got his story straight.

Fortunately there was enough traffic around for the car not to stand out. They would have the number, there was no question about that. There was little he could do about it, but as he knew the town so well it was easy to stick to side streets until he was out of it. Feeling more confident with every mile, he pulled into a self-service petrol station and filled the tank, making sure the registration number could not be seen on the security screen. With his hat tilted forward he went in to pay, using much-needed cash. He also bought a sandwich in a plastic packet and a carton of milk.

On the outskirts of Colchester he knew he must find somewhere to sleep and to dump the car, which he was going to report stolen. He left it in a car-park but did not purchase a ticket. On foot he found a pub and asked the thin-faced woman behind the bar if she knew anywhere that did bed and breakfast.

'How long for?'

'One night. I've got car trouble.' It was late, he didn't want to arouse suspicion.

'I'm the landlady, we can put you up here. Payment in advance.'

Smithy handed over the relevant sum, which left him with hardly any cash. 'Breakfast's at eight, is that all right?'

'Fine.' He had intended setting off early but it could be that Des went home for his lunch and he had no idea how long it would take him to get back by public transport. Better to leave it until after two.

He had a drink out of politeness because the woman thought she was doing him a favour by serving after she had called time. The effects of the earlier two had worn off and it might help him to sleep. In the cold bedroom he ate the sandwich and drank the milk from a glass on the shelf over the wash-basin. But sleep eluded him. If he was to report the car stolen he should have done it before now, because he was expected back that evening. He could say he'd spent the day doing something or other and was too tired to drive back and only discovered the car gone in the morning. But getting back in time for work would mean a very early start; he'd need to get up at six if his story was to sound genuine. Finally his eyes closed and he only woke when daylight filtered through the curtains. It was too late to make that call now.

Smithy ate a breakfast which could have been bigger then buttered a slice of toast, certain there was nothing to connect him with the three murders. Realisation dawned upon him: it

158

might be nothing to do with that at all, it could be that the police had wanted to see him about what happened with Marian. No, his brain told him, they do not sit outside your house for reasons as minor as that. He was going ahead with it. He had to kill Sheila. They wouldn't catch him – what reason did they have to think he wished her harm? They probably didn't even know of her existence. And there was that lovely snap of the baby on his mantelpiece which proved they were on good terms. He smiled to himself. Wouldn't Des be sick to think that Sheila had been keeping in touch with him behind his back!

He felt no sorrow or remorse for what he had done. That first one would be alive, he told himself, if she'd kept her mouth shut, and there was nothing to prove he'd ever been near the second one, nor the third, really, no proper record there either.

He was going to act innocent, he could do it, they had already had him in the station and he had got away with it then; no nerves, no nothing, they hadn't been able to spot it. He got up and went to the pay-phone in the corner. He knew immediately by Walker's voice that something was up – the police might even be there with him as he spoke. 'Where are you?' Walker asked, not sounding at all himself.

'I've had a few problems. Family matters. Sorry to let you down. Look, I'll be in touch later.' Smithy hung up. It was conceivable there was a tap on the line. Walker was straight, if the police weren't with him he would contact them immediately.

Smithy was right. For the second time in less than half an hour Walker rang the incident room.

He had to ask directions to the railway station but found he could get back to Rickenham Green quite easily, with only one change of train. And the police would assume he had made a run for it, they would be far less vigilant in the town itself, especially as they knew he had the car. There was the added confusion of its being found in Colchester if the car-park attendant was awake.

It was just before two as he approached the cul-de-sac where Des and Sheila lived. The T-shaped road was deserted, no cars and, hopefully, everyone out at work. He rang the bell of number 5. 'Yes? Can I help you?' A woman in her fifties smiled at him. Smithy had not expected anyone else to be in the house. It didn't matter, he was here now and he'd soon make Sheila get rid of the woman. He knew how to manipulate her and although it was three years since she left him he knew her well enough to understand she was still afraid of him. Why else have an ex-directory telephone number? Why else send that photograph anonymously, without any word whatsoever? Oh, yes, he knew why she sent it – to hurt him, to cause him more pain and grief than she had already done.

She was scared of him, of course she was, there was no other explanation for their moving away and keeping their whereabouts hidden from him. His obsession had overtaken him to the point where he no longer cared that this woman would be able to identify him, so sure was he that he would not be caught.

Smithy smiled back. 'I've come to see Sheila. I know she isn't expecting me, it's a surprise.'

'Oh, dear. Then you've come to the wrong address. There's no one called Sheila here, only me.'

'You're lying. ' He had seen a flicker of fear in her eyes. The bitch had talked about him. This had to be Des's mother. The woman's hands went up to her face in an automatic protective gesture as Smithy shoved the door wider and advanced towards her. He back-heeled the door closed in one swift movement. Pushing the woman to one side he called out, 'Sheila?', then again from the base of the stairs. He sensed, rather than saw, a movement. Spinning round he grabbed the woman's arm – she had been about to slip out of the front door. 'Oh no, you don't. Come on, we're going upstairs.'

Within a short time it was obvious Sheila was not in. He simply had not allowed for this, but he had the right house whatever this lying woman told him. There, in the second bedroom, was a small single bed with a Mickey Mouse duvet cover and a cot. On the windowsill were several soft toys.

'How do you explain this?' He indicated the room with a wave of the hand.

The woman frowned, unable to understand what he meant. 'It's for my grandchildren.'

'Grandchildren?' Smithy felt sick, it was worse than he imagined. Sheila had a second kid, one who had been born before she and Des were married. Staring at the woman he began to see a resemblance between her and her son and he hated her. 'Stop it!' he commanded as she began to cry. 'Downstairs. We'll wait. And you can get me a cup of tea and something to eat.'

'We've found where Des Cowan operates from, it's a small industrial estate in town. Someone from number three squad's on their way there now and they're tracing his home address. It's down to them now.'

'Thanks, Alan.' Ian wanted to be there, to be seen to be doing something, but had to content himself with leaving it to others. He had to be content to wait, and he was sick of waiting.

This time it paid off. Marian Thomas telephoned, unsure of whom to ask for, but when she said it was in connection with Robert Smith, the call was put through to the control room. 'I've remembered something else. I realise Mr Smith was less than honest with me, but he did say he used to live in Leicester. It's probably not true, but I thought I ought to let you know.' She was thanked accordingly and another force became involved in the case.

Smith, Ian knew, did not have a record but it was still worth checking locally because there were many things not on file or stored in a computer that the men on the streets knew, such as families who were 'trouble', the people who were always on the fringe of bigger things but were never actually arrested, and hundreds of other small snippets of information. They knew the ones who had got away and the wives of those who had not; they might, just might, know something about Robert Smith. If he had lived in Leicester.

It was more simple than that. Ian spoke to a senior officer. 'He worked here, but not for long – he was kicked out of the force.'

'It fits,' he told Barry. 'Smith did well in his training but once he was out there in his uniform his true colours showed. He was a power-seeker, liked intimidating people, especially women. A massive inferiority complex, it would seem.'

'It also explains explains how he's managed to keep one step ahead. However long he was there, he'd know the procedures and how not to leave any evidence.'

'His wife stuck by him through thick and thin, apparently, although some of his colleagues thought he gave her a rough time. And guess what? He's into martial arts. Come on, coffee.'

'Another?' But Barry knew it was a way of passing the time.

When they got back from the canteen they heard that Roger Walker's car had been found abandoned in a Colchester car-park, unlocked, but undamaged. Ian ground his teeth with impatience; according to the map this was not an indication that Smith was heading towards Oxford, unless it was by an extremely bizarre route.

Several things were taking place at the same time. Once they had Sheila Cowan's home address a team of officers was on its way. When the situation was explained to her, Sheila knew her worst fears had come true. Smithy had found them, and there was little Sam to worry about as well. Reassurance that several officers would be in the house at all times did little to alleviate her fear, they did not know her ex-husband. If or when he arrived, she was instructed to open the door and invite him in. She was in no danger, they would be waiting and listening. Sheila watched as they prepared the trap.

But no knock came.

Des Cowan employed another man now that his business

162

had taken off, and it was this man who was doing some welding when the police arrived. He told them where Des could be found, checking the address in the diary, then discovered he was to have some company while he worked – two men stayed with him in case it was Des Smithy was after.

Des wanted to return home immediately, unable to bear the thought of Sheila having to suffer any more on her own. He had married her because he loved her; it was his duty to protect her and the one time she needed him he was not permitted to be there. Instead he was taken back to his office where he cancelled the rest of the day's jobs, not caring if he lost business because of it. It was Sheila he couldn't bear to lose. 'How did he find us?'

'We don't know for certain that he has, Mr Cowan, and although we believe he was heading away from Rickenham, we can't take any chances.' Time was running on and it was beginning to look as if they were wrong, that Smith had gone into hiding, but they dared not leave Sheila Cowan on her own.

Mrs Bingham made a lop-sided cheese sandwich with shaking hands. Her initial terror had passed; she was a great believer in the theory that if someone intended harming you they did so immediately, not after they had eaten a sandwich, drunk a mug of tea and demanded a second sandwich. Her old resolve was restored and she began to wonder how to get herself out of the situation safely. She guessed that the man seated at her kitchen table had some sort of psychiatric disorder, that he was either paranoid or mistaking her for someone else. Had she known he had killed three women she might not have been able to act in so level-headed a manner when she was later required to do so.

'If he did take off yesterday he must have known we were on to him. But why mention Oxford at all, and why dump the car in Colchester?'

'Could've been stolen? OK, perhaps not.' Barry shrugged when he saw the expression on Ian's face. A criminal stealing a car, and then, in turn, having it stolen from him, was far too much like a coincidence for the Chief to contemplate.

'I think it's more like this. *If* we're right, and if he intends coming back, he probably used it as cover, to be able to observe without being observed. Don't forget, he'd know all the tricks. Or else he needed it for some sort of alibi, though please don't ask me what. But from what we know of him I believe he still thinks he's one step ahead of us.'

Barry refrained from pointing out that he was.

'You see, he may not know that we've traced Des Cowan's business address to Rickenham and that we know they live in Saxborough, therefore he may not be expecting us to keep a look-out locally. It's the old double bluff again, don't you see? Run off, have half the force in the county chasing after you, as they think, then turn up where you're least expected.'

'But why go at all? Or why risk coming back? That woman who lives behind Petals confirmed he did.' She had seen the car when she let her cat out but swore it was not there when she pulled her bedroom curtains over prior to getting undressed. But neither of them could come up with an answer.

They had discovered Des Cowan's business address without any difficulty and knew Smith would have done so too. They had to hope he had not yet found out where his ex-wife lived. At least she did not go out to work and their telephone number was unlisted. What they could not understand was why he had waited.

'Too bloody obvious,' Barry suggested. 'He wanted to throw sand in our eyes.'

'*If* it's his ex he's after.' That was the big if.

'Yesterday? It was fairly busy. I put in a new immersion heater first thing, then did a couple of small jobs. In the afternoon I serviced the central heating for a mate of mine, he runs a dress shop. Last thing I went to Sylvia Bingham's to

164

plumb in her washing machine. She's Sheila's friend's mother and she had given me the spare key because she was babysitting for her daughter.'

'You let yourself in?'

Des nodded, wondering what this policeman was driving at. 'It was perfectly all right, you can check with her, she trusts me.'

'Did you see anyone? Or a car?'

'Come to think of it, one did slow down but – oh, no, you don't think he thinks that's where we live? Sylvia! She might be in danger.'

'Are you expecting a call?' Smithy asked when the old-fashioned telephone jangled, startling them both.

'My daughter usually rings once a day, I expect it's her.'

So Des Cowan had a sister, he did not know that. 'Answer it then.'

Mrs Bingham lifted the receiver knowing perfectly well it was not Susan because she helped out at the playschool her oldest child attended two afternoons a week. She nodded as she listened and said yes twice and no once. Smithy grabbed the receiver from her and slammed it down. 'You lying bitch, that wasn't your daughter.' He struck her across the face. Mrs Bingham realised she had misjudged the man, he was still capable of violence, but she had been given some hope, and an ability she had inherited from her mother, that of never giving in no matter what the odds, saved her from a further attack.

'I didn't say it was my daughter, I said it probably would be. That was just some sort of telephone salesman, to do with loft insulation he said. I've already got it. If it goes again it *will* be my daughter because I'm not expecting any other calls. Oh.'

'What is it?'

'There's a man coming round this afternoon to measure up for new kitchen units.'

Mrs Bingham was immensely proud of herself. The police had rapidly ascertained that Smith was in the house and told her to invent an expected male visitor. She had taken it one stage further rather cleverly. She pointed out the washing machine, which was obviously brand new as it still had the sticky strip advertising the make stuck across the door, and the kitchen was in need of some decoration. The man, it seemed, believed her.

'All right, but when he comes you say you've changed your mind, you can't afford it or something. You are not to let him in.' But Smithy was becoming nervous. How much longer did he have to wait for Sheila to return?

'Ah, this must be the man from the kitchen centre.' Mrs Bingham walked confidently to the door, very much aware that Smith was just inside the living-room watching and listening and that he was near enough to grab her and use her as a hostage if necessary. Sensibly, she had given in and told him what he wanted to hear, that Sheila, whoever she might be, was her daughter-in-law and would be back later.

At first she thought the whole thing was a hoax, that what was happening was a continuation of the earlier horror. When she opened the door she did not have time to speak before she was pulled roughly outside and two men burst past her. She heard the sound of breaking glass, the window in the kitchen door she thought, because it was locked and the key not in it. It all happened so quickly she was unable to relate it with any accuracy when she went to stay the night with Susan to get over the shock. More men appeared from around the side of the house, the man Smith handcuffed between them. She did not think she had ever seen a man look so defeated; his head hung and he seemed inches shorter.

'He believed Sheila Cowan was married to my son and that I lived with them. Yes,' Mrs Bingham said to the next question. 'He only hit me the once but I was very scared.' But only now was she experiencing the onset of shock; now it was over and she was safe. 'He said he was going to kill Sheila and that neither I nor anybody else could stop him. I had no idea he

166

was talking about Sheila Cowan – if I had, well, I don't think I could have acted as if I didn't know who he was talking about. Thank God you arrived, he might've killed me instead.'

That possibility had crossed everybody's minds.

Des and Sheila were also in a state of shock, worse for Sheila as the tension had mounted as she waited for Smithy to knock at the door. She was unaware of his mistake, unaware that he had no idea they did not live in Rickenham Green but in Saxborough, only Des's business was there. And that was one of the reasons he had never seen Sheila out shopping.

She had not liked leaving Sam upstairs in the hands of a WPC but they could not risk taking him out of the house in case it was being watched. Even when he cried Sheila did not go up to him, not for one second would she endanger his life. But it was over now and they could start again, this time without any anxiety. In a day or two they would go over and see Mrs Bingham who, for the time, was staying with her daughter.

'It was close.' Barry said, once Smith was in custody.

'But it's not over yet.' He had not confessed but stuck to the story of going out for the day and the car being stolen.

'OK, I may have delivered flowers to those two women, but so what? Have you checked the books? Were they killed on the days I delivered?' It was his first mistake. Ian knew an innocent man would not remember the dates of two separate murders. Smith was too cocksure, he knew the dates did not coincide. For a gruelling length of time a question and answer session was in progress. Smith answered everything that was put to him, sometimes with the truth, sometimes with a lie.

And then he made a second mistake.

'All right, I can see your point, but just because I met the three women, doesn't mean I killed them.'

'Three women?' There was an expression of perfect satisfac-

167

tion on the face of DS Swan. They had only questioned Smith about delivering flowers to Beth Abbott, when he had come into contact with Debbie Orchard, and the roses to Carrie Griffiths.

'Well, it is three, isn't it? I do read the papers.'

'But you said, just because you'd *met* all three. Would you care to explain what you meant by that?'

Smith couldn't, but forensic evidence could. The van he used daily had been taken away for examination although they knew Roger Walker had been using it since his own car had disappeared – that, too, was now in the hands of the police. There was a lot of grit and dirt and, appropriately, petals but there were also a couple of cat hairs which matched those of Carrie's cat. This was not conclusive proof he had been in the flat, the cat might have come out and rubbed against his leg, but the map that Virginia Baxter had drawn was still in the compartment under the dashboard: this would have proved he had been to the house, even if Clive Baxter had not confirmed that the directions were in his wife's handwriting, because it was drawn as if they were standing in her doorway.

Piecing it all together, the likely explanation was that Smith had acted upon chances thrown his way. Debbie took in the flowers, saying he was lucky she finished work early on Wednesdays because it saved him a return journey. Beth Abbott's back gate was locked and it was not the policy of Petals to leave expensive bouquets on front doorsteps. Smith had returned the following week, using as an excuse the fact that he was in the area and wanted to make sure the lady in question had received her flowers. The messages on the Orchards' answering machine had been played back but the tape not rewound, therefore it seemed likely that she had gone into the lounge to stop the machine and Smith had followed her.

In Virginia Baxter's case it was as Ian suspected. Smith had been unable to find the address he was looking for and had already been sent the wrong way by a hiker. Noticing movement through the window he had either rung the bell or been

168

seen in advance by Mrs Baxter who then opened the door. To most people there was only one reason for a florist's van to pull into their drive. And Carrie, the recipient of roses from an ex-boyfriend, must also have said something along the lines of him being lucky to catch her at home as she did not start work until ten on Wednesdays. They did not know how he had gained entry and he refused to tell them even after he was charged.

It had been simple. Using a boxed orchid which was meant for another customer, he had gone to the flat at nine and said it was for her as she had been Petals' ten thousandth customer. He had grinned to himself when she said she was not usually lucky. He had taken the orchid away with him again, hidden in the pocket of his anti-static jacket.

'But the motive?' Ian shook his head. 'Did he decide to kill his wife when he did because he knew time was running out, that we were on to him, or was she to be his next victim anyway? I can see why he wanted her dead, but the others?' Sheila Cowan had admitted she sent the photograph with the intention of upsetting Smith, to pay him back for the years of brutality he had inflicted upon her and to show him that it was not her after all who was incapable of having children. 'To a man like Smith, with his inferiority complex and his bullying nature, it must have been a red rag to a bull.'

'The others were happily married and childless. Maybe some peculiar logic told him he was being altruistic, that he was saving their husbands from the same fate.'

But later they found out there was more to it. Brian Lord, police psychologist, had interviewed Smith – later still would come more psychiatric reports to be used as evidence when the case came to trial. Unless they had a confession by then.

'Very strange man, Ian,' Lord said as he stuffed his pipe with tobacco and blew clouds of obnoxious smoke into the air. It seemed not to bother him that there was a no-smoking policy throughout most of the building.

'At first it seems like the classic case; single parent family, brought up by his mother who may or may not have been married. She spoiled him and then, when it was too late, was unable to control him. Whoever spoke to her gave me the details. She said by the time he was sixteen she was terrified of him. Seems some time after that she got her brothers round and they threw him out, threatening to break every bone in his body if he ever returned. But there were problems before that. He was a bully in school. Still, he seemed to make some sort of effort, got a couple of jobs then, as you know, joined the force. Exemplary record to begin with.' Lord struck another match and held it to his pipe. Ian opened the window.

'He never got over being kicked out. He still blames the people he worked with – he told me he hadn't done anything wrong, it was some sort of vendetta. You see, he can't bear to be thwarted and I get the impression that this thing with his wife was not so much because he loved her but because she had the audacity to walk away from his violence. Had she gone back to him her life would've been hell, because she didn't, Smith had to kill her.'

'Is he mad?'

Brian Lord was not a man to use jargon, except when it was necessary. He did not correct Ian now. 'Who's to say? You could argue that anyone who kills cold-bloodedly is mad. But no, I don't think he is. We know he planned Debbie Orchard's murder, and that of Carrie Griffiths. Virginia Baxter died by chance, simply because he was lost that day, but each was significant to Smith – they were designed to lead you to think there was no pattern, that these murders were random and without motive.'

'You mean he deliberately killed three women to disguise the fact that he intended killing his wife?'

'Precisely that. To baffle you.'

'My God.'

More smoke belched out. 'At least, that's how he justifies it to himself.'

'Meaning what?'

'Meaning that I cannot put a label on the man, a nice, neat diagnosis. He might not be clinically insane but he is definitely, to use a layman's term, unbalanced. He has an inferiority complex bigger than I've ever known, it shows with his boasting, in his record with the Leicestershire police and the victims he chose. He picks on weaker people to prove to himself he's strong. Had he got to Sheila I don't think he would necessarily have stopped there, not as long as he was getting away with it. Anyway, you'll probably get much the same reaction from the rest of the shrinks.'

'Except they'll couch it in a more professional way.' Ian grinned.

'No doubt they will, dear boy. Now, the least you can do is buy me a pint.'

'That's supposed to be my line. Come on then, get your coat.'

'How did you get on to Cowan, by the way?'

'A chance comment. Someone said Smith might have lived in Leicester. Chap there remembered him, recalled his wife had left because of how he treated her, and he also remembered Des Cowan's name.'

'Quite a coincidence, him recalling the name.'

'No, it wasn't', Ian replied smugly.

'Oh?'

'The officer we spoke to at Leicester was also called Cowan. Now that *is* a coincidence.'

Brian Lord laughed loudly and deeply. He, too, knew the Chief's views on that subject.

'Let's say it's a belated birthday meal,' Ian said as he and Moira sipped their wine in the restaurant at the Elms Golf and Country Club, which was the most exclusive place to dine in Rickenham Green. And the most expensive. They had not gone out on the actual date and the holiday which should have compensated had not done so.

Under the chandeliers Moira's hair shone and seemed, to Ian, even lighter. He did not know she had put a rinse on it that evening. It was piled on her head, complementing the

171

flowing skirt and the soft folds of her blouse and, unusually, she looked more like a woman than a girl. 'We are all right, aren't we?' Ian asked as they waited for the main course to arrive.

'All right?'

'Yes. Us. You and me.'

She smiled. 'I've always been all right, Ian, it's you who gets into such a state about things. Besides,' the smile became a chuckle, 'how can you possibly think you've ever been all right? I'm not sure you're a hundred per cent there at times. And you know you live on a different planet from the rest of us. Good heavens,' the waiter was hovering over them, 'we'll never eat all this. Well, I won't.' Ian's appetite was an entirely different matter.

Conversation waned as the food took priority. 'No, nothing more,' Moira said later. 'It was delicious, but I'm really full. It's only nine thirty,' she added.

'So?'

'So if you want, we can call in at the Feathers and join the others.'

Ian's laugh caused the other diners in their hushed sur-roundings to glance round. How well Moira knew him. He had given up this night for her because he knew he owed it to her. And more. In turn, she appreciated it and realised that he had missed out on the celebrations with the rest of his team and that talking it over, which they inevitably would, was a sort of catharsis.

She lived to regret her decision. A few minutes after they arrived Lucy came to collect Barry and was persuaded to stay for a drink which led to her asking the landlord if she could leave the car in his car-park overnight. Alan Campbell and Winston Emmanuel were vying for the attention of Brenda Gibbons while Markham stood back and took it all in with an enigmatic smirk. It was Moira, who, because she was used to only a few glasses of wine, became bold and invited everyone back to Belmont Road for a nightcap.

In the morning they both overslept. Moira closed her mind

to Ian's grumbling as he poured the tea. She did not miss the slight tremor as he did so.

'There are more clean shirts in the airing cupboard. Go and change, I'll sew it on tonight,' she said sharply when the top button fell off his shirt. 'You've got blood on the collar anyway.' Last night at the Country Club had been a rare treat and an enjoyable one; this was normality. Moira realised there would be no such thing for the families of the victims for a very long time. 'Ian? What you were saying last night, about there being three murders before he tried to get to his wife. Perhaps there wouldn't have been any more.'

'What do you man?' He reknotted his tie and turned down the collar of a fresh shirt.

'She left him in January, didn't she? January three years ago. And that's when he received that snapshot and that's when he started killing. Do you think he wanted to take a life for each year of his own life Sheila had stolen from him?'

Ian paused, his hands still at his neck. 'I don't know, love. Perhaps we'll never know, or perhaps the shrinks'll find out in due course. God look at the time! Come on let's go.'

'I forgot to tell you,' she said when they were in the car and heading towards John Freeling's office, 'Mark's coming for the weekend and bringing a friend.'

Ian groaned. The thought of non-stop music, the base thudding overhead from Mark's bedroom, and heavy-footed youths up and down the stairs was more than he could cope with that morning. But Norwich was playing away on Saturday, he could escape for a few hours. He felt a twinge of guilt. Ipswich, the county team, were going down, he was glad he did not support them. But Norwich were also shaky.

'Morning, sir.' After a good night's sleep and a plate of bacon, egg and tomato and his wife's crispy fried bread, Sergeant Whitelaw was ensconced behind the desk in reception feeling good about life. What made him feel doubly good was the sight of several white-faced, haggard detectives dragging themselves unwilling in to work. The Chief nodded in greeting then winced, causing Sergeant Whitelaw to lower his eyes so he wouldn't see the gleam of satisfaction therein.

Serves the buggers right, he thought gleefully, remembering how little sympathy he had received the night after he and the wife had celebrated twenty-five years of marriage. It was the little things which made life worthwhile.